Acclaim for Eric Beetner's Rumrunners

"Buckle up...RUMRUNNERS is a fast and furious read."

— *Samuel W. Gailey, author of Deep Winter*

"Rumrunners just never lets up. It's a fuel-injected, mile-a-minute thrill ride from Eric Beetner. A violent crime-family saga with a sense of humor. I had a blast."

— *Grant Jerkins, author of A Very Simple Crime and Done In One*

"Few contemporary writers do justice to the noir tradition the way Eric Beetner does. Others try to emulate and mimic; Beetner just takes the form and cuts his own jagged, raw and utterly readable path. RUMRUNNERS is the latest example of his great storytelling skills, and his uncompromising commitment to the dark, often violent truth at the center of the human heart."

— *Gar Anthony Haywood, author of Assume Nothing, Cemetery Road and the Aaron Gunner series*

Rumrunners

Eric Beetner

Sam—
Thank you for the
kind words!

**280
STEPS**

1

There was a bullet hole in the window of the donut shop, pasted over with duct tape and an unevenly cut square of cardboard. It had been there ever since Calvin McGraw first came to the shop for a morning coffee and a glazed. But Calvin looked beyond the hole, an artifact from some long ago robbery. He didn't know how much they would have gotten away with from a donut shop heist. Not enough, he thought.

Instead, he watched the cars go by outside the greasy window. His 86-year-old eyes had barely lost any focus and he mumbled to himself with each passing ride, "Ford. Chevy. Ford. Chrysler. Goddamn Toyota."

His paper plate held only a sugary ring where his glazed had been, but his coffee was still tongue-scalding hot as he sat on the swivel stool and wasted another day. He didn't want to be watching cars, he wanted to be in them. Driving fast. Cops on his heels, sirens and gunshots in the air. Tires screaming, rubber burning, oil thrumming through a well-tuned engine like the blood pumping fast through his heart.

Like the old days.

Calvin still remembered. Running liquor through the Iowa

trees. Sneaking bales of pot across the river into Illinois. Driving anything and everything for the Stanley clan as they built their criminal empire, such as it was in a lonely southeastern corner of Iowa.

Even today he thought he got out of the game too early. He could still have been driving, like his son—in his sixties and still taking jobs. It wasn't about the money anymore. The goddamn Stanleys never paid that great anyway. It was about the smell of gasoline and the feel of a pedal when it hit the floor and couldn't go down any more.

Now here he was. Living in Omaha. How the hell did that happen?

Outside, past the streaks of sugar glaze blurring the window, one of those electric hybrid cars passed by on a whisper.

"Disgrace," Calvin said out loud.

"What'd you say to me?"

Calvin turned. A skinny man in his mid-twenties, but dressed like Calvin might have in the 1940s, glared at the old man.

"Nothing," Calvin said.

"No, you called me a disgrace. What did you mean by that?"

Ever since this place started making donuts with crazy-ass things like maple and bacon on them—bacon for fuck's sake—these downtown types who seemed to think they lived in Brooklyn, not in Omaha about as far away as you could get, had been taking all the stools and raising the price on a cup of joe.

"I didn't say it about you. I said it about the goddamn battery car that passed by."

"What's wrong with electric cars?"

Calvin rolled his eyes. He wanted to sit and watch his cars

in silence. Longing and regret about the past was a solitary hobby.

"Nothing other than everything. They're fuckin' stupid."

"I happen to drive a Prius."

"Of course you do." Calvin swiveled on his stool. He wasn't sure if the skinny guy was being bold because Calvin's age made him feel safe, but he was sure the guy had no clue who he was dealing with.

"Do me a favor," Calvin said. He curled his index finger twice to draw the man near. The hipster pushed his mustache closer, probably thinking the old man couldn't hear so well.

Calvin grabbed him by the middle finger. He pulled it back until it nearly touched the back of the man's hand. The man opened his mouth in a silent scream, too shocked to yell out. Or too embarrassed to be bested by an octogenarian.

"Listen kid," Calvin tugged the finger closer to breaking. "Just take your green tea dusted donut with quince paste filling and fuck off out of here. I'm drinking coffee and watching the cars go by. I ain't hurting you."

The skinny guy was down to one knee now, wincing in pain.

"Oh." Calvin looked at him. "I guess I am hurting you now. But I wasn't then."

He released the man's finger. The hipster exhaled like he'd been underwater. Nobody else in the shop noticed their tussle.

Calvin said, "So beat it, okay?"

"You're crazy. You could have broken my finger."

"Yes. I could have. And I didn't. Let's call that a win."

Cradling his wounded hand in his other, the man grew a pair of balls again and aimed his angry mustache at Calvin. "I can have you arrested, you know."

"I guess you didn't get the message, son."

Calvin snatched the man's good hand, twisted his index finger while jerking up on it. Felt the pop. This time, the guy screamed.

Calvin lifted his coffee cup. Still hot. He walked out.

2

"Webb, got a big one for you." Hugh Stanley didn't call many people directly, but when you'd known an employee and his family since the day you were born you made an exception. Webb's father Calvin had driven Hugh's mom to Mercy Hospital to deliver the boy in a snow storm an early January morning in 1958. Webb was six years old and helped his dad wipe down the back seat afterward, soaking up all the fluid she dumped when her water broke. Didn't smell like no water to Webb.

"Thank Christ you called, Hugh," Webb said. "I was beginning to think you all forgot about me."

"You know how it is, Webb. Things are slow."

"Yeah, yeah. The economy and all that shit. Isn't that when people do more illegal substances? Crime goes up? Shit like that?"

"Look, I got a doozy for you. You want it or not?"

"I want it."

The Stanley family would have liked to think they ruled over a vast criminal empire but really they just happened to be the biggest fish in a very small pond. Running anything and everything illegal was all the Stanleys had known for nearly a hundred years.

And all along the McGraws had driven for them. Like one of those remora fish attached the underbelly of a shark, a McGraw had been swimming along with the Stanley clan for almost a century.

Webb McGraw was the last one. His boy, Tucker, wanted no part in the driving business. Just as well. Didn't have the nerve for it.

Webb was getting up in years, but still he was the man to call when a Stanley needed a driver. And not some chauffeur around town open-the-door-for-you bullshit. It might not be the thrill-a-minute days of running liquor through the backwoods, but plenty of things got shipped that you wouldn't call FedEx for.

"This one will set you up for quite a while," Hugh said.

"Well, color me curious, boss. Whacha got?"

"A certain shipment from a certain pharmaceutical company has been, shall we say, lost en route. I need you to go get it and bring it to me."

"Alright. What about the boys who found the lost items?"

"Intermediaries. Don't want them too close to this one, lest they get big ideas."

"I see."

Webb stayed true to one of the cardinal rules for driving— never ask what the cargo is. Doesn't matter if it's a ton of heroin or a ton of candy canes. You do the job, deliver the goods, say goodbye.

This one, however, was too good for Hugh to keep to himself.

"You know how meth has been our growth industry lately?"

"Lately being the last fifteen years, yeah." The Midwest was the birthplace of trucker's speed and now the whole damn country was off the high falutin' booger sugar of the cities and deep into the hick high of crystal meth. That and corn. Iowa had it all.

Hugh continued with an excitement in his voice like his teenage granddaughter talking about the latest pop music haircut with a record deal.

"We got a whole shipment of pseudoephedrine. Straight from the factory. A whole mountain of the stuff."

"That's big time."

"You better believe it. This one score will keep us in the pink for three years, I figure."

"My usual cut?" Hugh had blown any chance to lowball Webb on this one.

"For your trouble, twenty-five g's. How's that grab you?"

"Wish I got grabbed like that a lot more. When and where?"

Hugh gave him an address across the river in Illinois, then almost derailed the whole affair. "You can drive a big rig, right?"

Webb hoped the boss man didn't notice the pause before, "Sure. No problem."

An eighteen-wheeler? Hell no, he couldn't drive that. Webb grew up a muscle car guy. American only. Hated the feeling of anything less than eight cylinders under his feet, but always four wheels and only four. He didn't go the other way and do motorcycles. But a big rig?

For twenty-five grand, he'd learn.

***

There were very few pleasantries whenever Tucker's father called him. He knew he'd turned out to be a big disappointment to Webb. No aptitude for driving, no interest in a criminal lifestyle, hated watching NASCAR.

"You know stock car racing was born out of bootlegging, don't you? Your granddaddy practically invented the sport."

"Yes, Dad." Sigh. "I know."

Reminding Webb how many times he'd told that story was beside the point. Webb knew he'd explained it hundreds of times before. The kid wasn't getting it. This was him. This was who he was. It was all in there and Tucker refused to let it out. The real McGraw inside him lived as a prisoner in solitary.

Tucker ignored his dad as easily as he ignored the caged DNA animal inside.

"Tucker, you know anyone who's a trucker?"

Tucker heard his dad snigger on the other end of the phone, amused by his own alliteration.

"A truck driver? No, Dad. I don't."

"Shit."

"Why?"

"'Cause I'm looking for one."

Seven phone calls and about a dozen layers of referrals later he found a guy who knew a guy who worked with a guy who did a favor for someone or other who owed some money to Webb.

How the fuck could it be so hard to find a truck driver? Freaking highways were littered with 'em.

**

When they met up outside Moline, IL. neither one could

unravel the knot that tied them together. They decided to hell with it, the five grand Webb was paying sure smelled good and this guy, Lonny, could drive a truck and that was that.

"So what are we hauling?" was the first question out of Lonny's mouth after he got in the car next to Webb.

Webb turned to look at him. Fat gut hanging out a good six inches over a longhorn steer belt buckle, thinning hair at the top that tapered off into a wispy pony tail in back, black T-shirt under an open red checked flannel. Yep. A trucker all right.

"We don't ask that."

"What do you mean?"

"It don't matter what's inside. We get in, drive it to the destination and take our check. You always know what you're hauling?"

"Yeah, I do. I got it on the manifest."

"Well, no manifest for this one."

For the forty minute drive Lonny's mind wandered to wild speculative places. Guns. That was his first assumption. Arming some militia out in the sticks against the government or the zombie apocalypse, whichever descended first.

Human trafficking. A trailer's worth of Russian prostitutes or central American workers. Lonny lingered a little longer on the vision of the prostitutes.

Eventually the curiosity gnawed at him like a chigger under his skin.

"I can't do the job if I don't know what I'm hauling."

Webb nearly drove into a ditch. "What do you mean?"

"You offer me five grand to drive a rig and you won't tell me what's in it? It don't smell good. Might be the risk isn't worth five grand."

"I knew it. You bucking for a raise?"

"No. I just want to know what I'm hauling so I know how to proceed."

The timetable had already begun. Webb was due back in Iowa by morning and it took too damn long to find this lazy trucker. Protocol had to be broken.

"It's a shipment of unprocessed drugs used to make methamphetamine. The stuff they use to make cold medicine, only before it gets put into the pills and shit. That's about all I know about it except that it's worth a shit load of money and we need to get the load back to my employers by the A.M. Is that enough for you?"

Lonny's eyes went glassy, lost in thought again. He never would have guessed.

"Yeah, sure. Okay. I'll do it."

"Damn right you will."

The rig sat parked behind a self-storage unit. Two skinny twenty-somethings in hooded sweatshirts and jittery limbs waited by the back of the trailer, twin orange dots from their cigarettes glowing.

Webb parked the car, watched the two kids he was to meet and figured they'd be using a little of the product they were helping to make. No matter what profit they made from their little truck-jacking, most of it was going right back to the Stanleys for powder to put up their nose. Ah, the circle of life.

Webb saw Lonny eyeballing the truck. "Can you drive it?"

"Yep."

"Then let's go."

The two orange dots hit the ground and were crushed underfoot. "Where the fuck you been?" The taller of the two oozed smoke as he talked.

"Driving. Where you been?" Webb countered. Sixty-four years old and he could still bring a cement hard attitude to a meeting if needed.

"We been here freezing our asses off."

"It's not even cold out. You should put a little meat on your bones."

"What, like this fat fuck here?" he said gesturing to Lonny.

"Why don't we make this happen so you can get out of here and go soak in a warm tub or some shit."

"Alright, alright. You wanna check it?"

"Nope." Webb moved his eyes between the two tweakers. "If it's not all there the Stanleys will know it and they'll send someone else out. You know what that means, so I won't go all school teacher and spell it out for you."

The two men shifted on their feet. It looked like they were about to start a two on two basketball game except Webb and Lonny remained flatfooted.

"I wanna see it," Lonny said.

Webb shot him a look like, didn't you hear what I said?

"I always check my load against the manifest."

"I told you there isn't any—"

Webb heard the metal scrape of the trailer door rolling up. The skinny silent one had pushed open the back and now shone a mag light into the trailer. It wasn't filled top to bottom with cargo but there were two long stacks on either side leaving an aisle up the middle. Boxes were stacked three high. Webb had a flash vision of the ending to Raiders of the Lost Ark.

Lonny's eyes wouldn't have been any more hungry than if it had been those Russian hookers.

"Okay, looks good. Shut it now." Webb tried to hustle it along. All three of the men in his company made him nervous.

Skinny boy jumped up and grabbed hold of the strap then leapt off the tailgate and used his slight body weight to draw down the roll door. It slammed shut like a prison cell.

"You'll be contacted with payment. Keys?"

The tall one tossed out a single key on a ring. Webb raised a hand to catch it but Lonny intercepted the missile instead.

Webb caught his eye. "We good?"

"Oh yeah, real good."

Webb saw him spending that five grand already behind his eyes. More belt buckles, probably.

"What about your car?" the tall one said. "Someone coming to collect that too?"

"Keep it," Webb said. "It's stolen."

The rig started right up and after an awkward left turn to make it out of the storage lot they were headed back toward Iowa and Lonny already found a country station on the radio. The driver's side window had been left open and the cab had a chill, but the heater worked fine and Lonny seemed to be enjoying the nearly-new condition of the Peterbilt. He rolled the window up and noticed a smear as he did. Something on the weather stripping around the window that streaked as he cranked it back into place. Something red. He cranked the gearbox up another as they gained speed toward the highway, then Lonny reached out and touched the smear. He checked his fingers.

Blood.

He showed the stain to Webb who shrugged his shoulders. He sure didn't figure it was those two kids who drove the big rig out there in the first place. Some poor sucker on his night shift drew the short straw and ended up hauling the wrong cargo.

The after midnight traffic on the interstate moved a steady five miles over the limit. There wasn't much to be said so Webb and Lonny let the country crooners do all the talking.

Webb breathed a little easier once they were back across the river and into Iowa. Illinois never quite felt right to him. Something about that state felt like a kid who'd been dropped on his head as a baby. There was something... off about it.

When his body relaxed Webb realized how badly he had to piss.

"Hey, pull off the next stop. I gotta take a leak."

"Yeah, I don't see any trucker's friends in here."

"A what?"

"Empty bottle you can pee in."

"Jesus Christ, you do that?"

"You get real good at taking out your prick at highway speeds."

Webb shook his head.

Lonny piloted the rig into a space along a row of other trucks parked and idling.

"Hey, grab me a Mountain Dew in there," Lonny said.

"You don't need to piss?"

"Nah. Got a bladder of steel."

"Okay." Webb hopped down out of the cab. He dodged oil stains as he walked across the lot to the brightly lit mini mart and fast food combo.

Easiest twenty grand I ever made, he thought. I don't even have to do the driving.

More country music assaulted his ears inside, but he could tolerate some whiny twang for the next hour it would take for the truck to be delivered.

After an epically long piss he bought two Mountain Dews and wove between more oil slicks on his way back to the truck.

Looking at the long line of sleeping cabs, yellow running lights on and heaters, TVs and DVDs of porn starring chubby girls playing inside, he felt a wave of nausea. The fumes didn't help, but it was the realization that he left Lonny unsupervised with the stash.

His brain made a logical justification out of the illogical idea that Lonny couldn't take off with the load because he didn't have the address where it was being delivered. Only now did Webb see that if Lonny was going to make off with the rig he would go anywhere but the meeting place.

He gripped a can of Mountain Dew in each hand and began running. The backs of all the trailers looked the same. One truck was a moving van with a bright green logo on the trailer so that wasn't it. His truck had almost no markings at all. It was generic. Easily lost. Easily hidden.

Webb hadn't run in quite a while and thoughts of a heart attack now flooded his brain with the influx of fast moving blood. Pressure was building inside the cans of soda as he pumped his arms and ignored the spots of oily ground, his eyes skimming from one trailer to another, all of them blending into one anonymous truck barreling past on the highway.

A lifetime in service to the Stanleys and this was how it ended. Webb would finally be the one to bring disgrace to the McGraws. Losing a few cases of liquor for his dad would have been a hanging offense. Losing an entire big rig full of unprocessed meth? Webb's mind didn't even know of a punishment to suit the crime.

A sound penetrated the pounding thoughts. A high lonesome wail. Country music. Webb stopped. He turned to his right, looking at the tractor trailer he stood behind. It had no markings. Plain. He followed the sound.

Inside the cab the tunes were cranked and a tin-eared trucker sang along. Sounded like he was celebrating something.

Webb hoisted himself up on the running board of the cab and saw Lonny belting out a tune, big 'ol smile on his face.

Webb exhaled, felt his blood pressure drop fifty points. Better than leaving a hundred Illinois' at once. He opened the cab door and slid in, trying to catch his breath.

Lonny didn't turn down the music or stop singing. He took the can of Mountain Dew. "Thanks!" he shouted over the song. Webb wasn't sure, maybe Willie Nelson?

Before Webb had his answer he was falling backward out of the cab. The tire iron hit him square between the eyes. That smile never dropped off Lonny's face.

He tumbled down and hit the cool asphalt, hard. He already tasted blood from the split in his skin across the bridge of his nose. The can of Dew split and sprayed like champagne mocking him.

The sound of the engine coming to life was a T. Rex, King Kong and a Terminator all rolled into one. Webb slid back away from the tire as the gears clawed into reverse like teeth gnashing at meat. The truck began to move and Webb reached out a hand but it only brushed against the front tire as the eighteen-wheeler rolled away.

3

There was a war inside Webb McGraw. Fess up or fuck off were the two sides. The battle had been fierce.

After hitching a ride with a friendly trucker who wanted neither cash nor a blow job for his trouble, Webb arrived back at home base with a choice to make. Tell the Stanleys they weren't getting their truck or split town and do what he did best—drive. And keep on driving.

There was always the nuclear option—the elaborate lie. Webb never was much for lying. Always too worried he'd get caught to commit to a tall tale. He'd seen too many people over the years get caught out in a lie and pay the price in more ways than he could count. From cash money to digits of the finger and toe kind—to life itself.

No, better leave the lying to the pros. He was a grease monkey, Richard Petty wannabe, lead foot McGraw like his dad and granddad before him. It wasn't like them to run, but in his experience it wasn't like the Stanleys to do a whole lot of sympathetic understanding either.

He landed home about 4:30 in the morning, made a pot of coffee and sat in his empty house to think. No wife. She was cooling in the ground about five miles away under a tombstone built for two waiting for Webb to come home. Tucker, his only child, hadn't been to visit in over a year.

No, Webb faced this dilemma alone. On his second cup of coffee he noticed he hadn't been spiking it with bourbon. A subtle sign, but a sign nonetheless. He never drank on driving nights. Somehow his body knew he wasn't done driving for the evening.

In his car, his favorite car—the 1970 Plymouth Barracuda—on his way to see Hugh Stanley he almost banged a U-turn at every intersection he drove through. Integrity got the best of him. The closer he got, though, the harder it was to keep the wheel on the straight and narrow. It didn't help his nerves any to be parking out front of the Stanley compound at six A.M.

It was 6:30 by the time he stepped out of the car. His finger hovered over the call button at the gate. His name would gain him entry at any hour, but anyone arriving unannounced and this early would get an armed escort to the door. After that, Webb had no idea what could be in store. All his ideas gave him a headache. All Hugh Stanley's ideas, or one of his shitbag sons, were sure to give him a headache of a very different kind. The 9mm kind. The chainsaw kind. The back tire of his own Barracuda backing up over his melon kind.

Last chance, Webb, he thought. Nothing holding you here except steady employment that had grown not so steady lately. Tucker wouldn't give a shit if you up and left town. Maybe head out to Omaha and see Dad. Calvin, the old bastard still kicking ass and taking names.

That finger hovered like a mosquito waiting for a fat vein.

4

Tucker burned the pizza. Always going for the extra brown on the cheese like the picture on the box. Dinner was served. The freezer offered little else in the way of second prize, so blackened pepperoni pizza it was.

While it cooled in the kitchen, Tucker set up a tray in front of the TV. He'd bought the set of four when he and Jenny were still married. He saw the gesture as an attempt at family togetherness, she saw it as the opposite. An admission of defeat.

"We can't even sit at a goddamn dinner table any more?"

"Well, I don't know. Milo just watches TV over our shoulders anyhow. I figure we could all sit together and watch some programs for families like that Survivor or something."

"Don't give me any ideas about running off to a desert island."

"It's not like it's a vacation for those people. It's hard, you know."

Jenny bore down on him with one of her stares. Her eyes, pretty as they were, burned like twin soldering irons sometimes.

The knock at the door caught Tucker before he could retrieve his charred pizza.

The man at the door did not immediately intimidate. He came alone, wore a tie and button-down shirt under his tasteful leather jacket. He held no weapon and made no move to enter Tucker's home and yet Tucker was still scared right away.

"Mr. McGraw?" the stranger began.

"Yes." Tucker held firm to the edge of the door in a pudding-tough attempt at keeping the man out.

"I'm Kenny Stanley. You father works for us from time to time."

He knew the name. "Yes?"

"May we have a word?"

Tucker thought they were having a word, but what the young Stanley meant was could he come inside and dump a truckload of shit all over his house that would take maybe the rest of his life to clean up. But Tucker knew the name and what the name meant so what else could he do?

"Come in."

He stepped aside and Kenny walked in with the confidence of a boss over an employee.

"What's this about?" Tucker asked, declining to offer his guest any pizza.

"I was wondering if you'd heard from your father at all."

"We talk from time to time."

"In the last forty-eight hours?" Kenny surveyed the living room with the meager light provided by the single bulb floor lamp and the glow of the muted TV playing Jeopardy.

"Not in about six weeks. Why?"

"We can't seem to raise him either and he has something

of ours. One of his jobs for us. He never made his delivery."

"I don't know anything about it." This was just the sort of visit that kept Tucker far away from the family business all his life.

Kenny grinned with an insincere reptile curl of the lip. "Your family and my family have been in business together for a long time." Kenny let the statement of fact hang in the air to mix with the charcoal smell of the burnt pizza. "No McGraw has ever missed a delivery. Especially not one of this size."

"I'm sorry, but I don't know anything about my dad's business. I don't have anything to do with it."

"But, you are a McGraw, right?"

"Yeah. Just not that kind of McGraw."

"Well, as the next of kin—"

"What? Is my dad... dead?" The meeting had quickly turned into the other sort of visit that kept Tucker out of the business.

"We don't know. He's gone is all we do know. No one at his house. His car gone and, more importantly, our cargo gone."

More importantly? Than a man's life? Tucker had every reason in the world to hate the Stanleys. Add one more.

"What was your cargo?"

"That's not important. It was large and very valuable. Those are the key items." Kenny sounded like he either had one year of law school before he dropped out or he watched a lot of TV.

Tucker had a thought. "He did call the other day." Kenny perked up. "Only for five seconds which is why I forgot. He asked if I knew any truck drivers."

"Truck drivers?"

20

"I don't."

"I see."

"That was it, though. I never heard what he wanted someone like that for."

"To drive a truck, I assume." The cold-blooded smile came back to Kenny's lips.

"Anyway, that was the last time I talked with him."

"Uh-huh." Kenny spread his legs shoulders wide like a soldier at ease. "Like I was saying, as the next of kin and me acting as my daddy's representative, I have to ask you now for your father's debt to us."

All three contestants on Jeopardy got the final answer wrong. Some guy won the whole shebang with a hundred bucks in the bank. Tucker was faring no better in coming up with an answer to why this jackass was in his house.

"Excuse me?"

"To put it simply, the debt transfers down. Your father has fucked us for a large sum of money. Money you now owe." The even keel of his tone stretched even more even, giving it a threatening tautness.

"I can't... I mean, why should I owe you any money?"

"Because your father owes us money and we can't find him."

"So go look for him. I can't help you."

"We can find ways for you to help us."

Tucker sat back onto the couch. "You can't be serious."

"I'm a Stanley. We're always serious."

Silence enveloped the room thicker than a bad first date. Tucker kept waiting for Webb to jump out of the shadows and announce his big practical joke. When no one did any jumping Tucker began to get angry at Webb for bringing him

21

into a life he'd told his dad he wanted no part of. Tucker knew the infectious nature of a life of crime and wanted to keep himself fully stocked in penicillin against his own dad and anyone like him.

"How much?"

Kenny displayed some of that famous Stanley seriousness. "Ten million."

"What?" This had to be a joke now.

"And that's being generous. Years of service have to be worth something."

"You expect me to come up with ten million dollars?"

"Yes, we do. Unless you can return our merchandise. Then we'll call it even."

"Oh, call it even. How nice. Do you have any idea who you're talking to? Look around you. I sell insurance. My ex-wife takes half my paycheck. I'm about to eat my fifth frozen pizza in as many days because they were on sale last week at the store, so I bought a week's worth. How the hell am I gonna get you ten million dollars?"

"I have no idea. But, I'll be back to collect it."

"It won't be here."

"Then you'd better find your father."

There it was. He didn't really expect Tucker to come up with that amount of money. The Stanleys were using it as leverage to make Tucker dig up his dad. The cash might have been easier to find.

"Let me tell you something," Tucker said. "He's much more likely to take your call."

Kenny moved toward the door, never having made himself comfortable in Tucker's house, if that was even possible.

"Like I said before, we're being generous because of your

family name. We don't want to think the worst of a McGraw. Maybe there's a simple explanation for all this."

Tucker stood. "I'm sure there is."

"Until we find out what that is, ten million. Good night. Enjoy your pizza."

Kenny opened the door and let himself out. Tucker stood in the gloom of his living room trying to get the joke.

Final Jeopardy answer: a lot. Question: How fucked am I?

5

"Tucker who?"

"Your grandson. Your only grandson." Granted, Calvin hadn't spoken with Tucker in at least three years, but to not even recognize his only grandchild's name?

"Oh, shit, yeah. How the hell are you, boy?" Calvin came across the line from Omaha clear as lake ice. The gravel in his voice only faked his age. That rough road of a voice box had been that way for decades.

"Dad's gone missing."

"Who's dad?"

"My dad. Your son. Webb."

"You don't say?"

Tucker slapped an open palm to his forehead. "I do say, Granddad, and the Stanleys say too. They came around here asking me to pay for something he stole on his way out of town."

"Stanleys, you say?"

"Yeah. The Stanleys."

"Sons a bitches. Been using us McGraw men like slaves for eighty years. Never once looked on us as any more than

24

chauffeurs and errand boys. Fuck 'em.'"

"Well, Granddad, I can't exactly eff them. They want money from me. And I don't know where Dad is. Have you heard from him?"

"Not in a few weeks. Stole something you said?"

"Yes. A delivery he was making."

"Bullshit. No McGraw would ever steal cargo. Hold tight. I'll be right there."

A trip across the flat cornfield carpet between Omaha and Iowa City took most people about four hours. Calvin showed up in two and a half. The original lead foot. His dad, Edgar, never lived long enough to see a car with three hundred horsepower. Would have wept like a baby to be behind the wheel of a ride like that.

When his grandfather arrived at Tucker's house he looked like a returning soldier. Calvin's face glowed with the wind-blown top-down aura only high speed night driving could accomplish. He walked straight and with purpose to his grandson, a thick hand extended out before him.

"Put 'er in the old vice, kid." Vice is about right. He pumped Tucker's hand up and down, squeezing until the bones ached and knocked against their neighbors. McGraw men don't hug.

"Hope I'm not too late for the wife and kid."

"They don't... we're separated. About three years now, actually."

"Goddamn. Sorry as shit to hear it, Tuck. Goddamn. McGraw men don't get divorced, we outlive our wives. My dad, your dad, me."

"Yeah, well. First time for everything."

Tucker ran down what he recalled about his conversation

with Kenny.

"Ten million?" barked Calvin. "They're fucking with you."

"I don't think they are. I think they wanted to light a fire under me to help find my dad. He didn't set a specific timetable. Just said he'd be back."

"Which one was it you say?"

"Kenny."

"Hmm, don't know him. Been a while I guess. Hell, I ain't even seen my own great-grandson in a coon's age. How is the boy?"

"With his mom. Can we focus here?"

Calvin eyed Tucker with a judgmental look, assessing some kind of weakness in a man who would let his ex-wife take away his only son. With a shake of his head Calvin finished the can of Pabst Tucker gave him the moment he walked in.

"Got any more?" Tucker went to the fridge to get another round for Calvin. He stuck with water for himself.

The forced bachelor squalor of Tucker's house didn't bother Calvin. He'd been a widower for twenty-seven years and his place in Omaha would take a bulldozer and a hazmat team to clear out. Retirement hadn't agreed with him. Still spry and in shape he spent time fidgeting around the house like a teenager low on Ritalin. The tank-and-a-quarter blast across Iowa to get there had been the most fun he'd had in years.

"I'll tell you one thing, Webb didn't steal nothing and he didn't run off. He wouldn't do that. He was a McGraw through and through. We don't disrespect the job that way."

"Then where is he?" Tucker had been avoiding the D word since Kenny arrived at his door. If Calvin said it, or at least brought up the possibility, it might lessen the blow.

"I don't know. But I aim to find out." Calvin drained the

second beer. "That ought to help me hit the hay. What do you say we pick this up in the morning and find out a few things?"

Tucker checked his watch. 12:30. No other 86-year-old man in the state was still awake. With visions of his dad dead on a roadside and a pile of ten million dollars about to topple over and crush him, Tucker knew he wouldn't get much sleep tonight. Something about having Calvin there made him feel a little better though.

Calvin lifted his feet and began pressing his body into the couch cushions.

"Granddad, you can have the bed. I'll take the couch."

"Couch is good enough for me. Don't you worry."

Tucker brought him a blanket from the hall closet.

"Thanks, kid." For the first time since he arrived, he looked old. "Good to see you."

Tucker smiled, but it faded quickly. "Good to see you, too."

Calvin looked back at him with a stare only years could bring. "You want me to tell you it's all going to be fine, don't you?"

Tucker turned his head down, fighting off a wave of embarrassment. "It'd be nice."

"I'm not gonna. Them Stanleys are good, upstanding business people who may have treated us like the help, but always treated us square. But let's not forget what business they're in. And these young kids now taking over, they don't have the same length of memory. Might be your dad isn't treated with the respect he deserves. But I mean what I say when I say he didn't steal nothing. No truck. No drugs. Whatever it is, no son of mine ever turned crooked and ran."

Tucker's head might have thought his father capable of anything criminal or unsavory, but his heart knew Calvin

27

was right. Webb operated under a strict code of ethics in an unethical profession. It made the alternative harder to stomach.

"G'night, Granddad."

"G'night, kid. Nice to see you got some of the McGraw code of honor in you yet. Might be you can't drive worth a shit, but you know never to leave a man behind."

"He's my dad."

"And he's my son. And we're gonna find him."

6

Calvin scratched his balls as he stepped into the kitchen, his white hair at kinky angles from his night on the couch. He ignored Tucker and went straight for the fridge, pulled the last can of Pabst from the plastic rings and cracked the top.

"I made coffee, y'know," Tucker said, offering a mug.

Calvin took the cup by the handle, looked at the beer, then the mug, then the beer, back to the coffee. He took a long pull on the beer can, swallowed deep, set it on the counter and followed with a coffee chaser.

A loud knock rattled the door. Calvin halted the coffee mug half way to his lips as he and Tucker shared a look.

"Stanleys?" asked Tucker.

Calvin set the mug down next to the Pabst. "You got a piece?"

"A piece of what?"

"A gun, you fool."

"No."

Calvin shook his head like the boy had admitted he couldn't change a tire.

"Go on ahead," Calvin said.

Tucker walked to the door. Calvin stayed behind, hiding his body in the doorway to the kitchen which gave him a partially obstructed view of the front door. No way the Stanleys would be so dumb as to come back the very next day to make their claim, and no way they'd come in guns blazing without some talk first. This was not a vengeful clan, they'd rather have the cash.

Tucker opened the door to Jenny, his ex. Tall, blond with boobs barely two years old and still smelling of that boyfriend who wasn't much older. Ron. Jerk-off smoked menthols like a high school girl.

Tucker felt the same tugs, like marionette strings, to his heart, his stomach. The flush to his face. The torch he still held for her burned him every time.

"Jenny," Tucker said with genuine surprise.

"What the hell is that?"

"What's what?"

"That." She pivoted her hips and pointed to Calvin's convertible 1980 Trans Am, his dream car. The Smokey and the Bandit car. The fruits of Calvin's labor. "Did you get a goddamn new car?"

For a woman who cheated and left him, Jenny was a shit to Tucker.

"No. That's not my car."

She narrowed her eyes. "Do you have a woman in here? In my house?"

"Okay, a few things. One, it's not your house. Two, I don't have a woman in here and even if I did it's none of your concern and three, it's my granddad's car and he's here for a visit."

Calvin faded back around the doorjamb, not wanting the

she-devil to spot him.

"Oh." Jenny's anger had no place to go. She strained for a direction to aim her momentum. "How is Calvin?"

"Good. He's good. He was asking after Milo. Wanted to see him."

"Milo's grounded. He skipped school again. Third time this month. That boy, Tucker... that boy. He needs a talking to."

"I wish you'd let me then. This every other weekend crap doesn't exactly lend itself to a close father-son relationship. He doesn't tell me things anymore. He's at the age when he doesn't want to tell anyone over age thirty a damn thing about his life."

She thrust out a hip and her bracelets rattled as she planted a hand on her jutted out midsection. "You expect me to increase your visitation without you increasing your monthly payments? No judge is gonna agree to that."

"Why do we have to get judges involved? Can't we just be his parents? If the boy needs something, if he's drifting, let me help."

"I don't know, Tucker. I just do not know. Look, I don't have time to argue about this now. I was driving by and saw the car and I thought..."

"You thought I was holding out on you and buying myself toys."

She at least had the decency to look ashamed. "Something like that."

"Believe me, Jenny, you get every last cent that's left over each month. I'm not going to be buying any new cars any time soon."

"Okay." She did her best to peek around Tucker and make sure no women were hiding under the couch or behind the potted plants. "Say hi to Calvin for me."

"I'll do that. Would you tell Milo his granddad wants to see him?"

"Okay. Maybe y'all can get a Dairy Queen together or something while I go to the gym."

"That'd be nice." Tucker realized his definition of what would be 'nice' had eroded over the years.

The high tick-tick-tick of Jenny's heels faded away as she walked down the driveway, eyeballing the Trans Am.

Calvin stepped out from the kitchen, coffee mug back in his hand. "Quite a reunion there."

"That was about average."

"What's she on about with the money?"

"Alimony. My monthly bill. Her lawyer went after me during the divorce and it happened at a high point in the insurance game. People buying homeowners policies for houses they shouldn't have ever been in. People with extra money to spend on some peace of mind. Nowadays people spend their extra money on stuff like food and clothing. They set my monthly payment at a time when I made more money than I ever had. Now the judge won't hear my appeal to get it reduced to match my salary 'cause my base salary is the same, but it was the bonuses and commissions that made the difference. Those are all gone."

Calvin sipped his coffee, shook his head. "A goddamn shame."

"I know. The whole system is—"

"A McGraw man hard up for cash."

"Well, it's the whole industry really. It's—"

"You're pissing away your gift, boy. Selling insurance. What the hell is that?"

"It's a decent, honest living."

"It's a cemetery plot with a business card. It's an iron lung with a company car. It's a slow suicide by bus bench advertisements. And it's a waste of valuable resources. McGraw blood is meant to be coursing through a V-8, not an actuary table. Yes, I know what that is."

"I'm not a criminal."

"Bullshit. What you're doing with your own blood is the biggest crime I know."

Calvin turned and went back to the kitchen. Tucker followed. Calvin set the coffee mug in the sink, picked up the can of beer, upended it and slurped down the last drops. The can thunked empty on the tile countertop. "Let's get going."

Tucker waited for the Trans Am's engine to quiet from the revs after Calvin started her up.

"Where are we going exactly?"

"Sounds like you need a little dough."

Tucker sat up in his seat, reacting like he'd been told the roller coaster he was on didn't have brakes. "I'm not going to steal it."

"Neither am I. There's a guy who owed your dad some money. We'll go see him."

"Who?"

"A guy."

"How do you know about it?"

"I actually talk to my son."

The Firebird squealed tires away from the curb. Somewhere Jerry Reed was singing East Bound and Down.

***

The farmhouse sat with fifty acres between neighbors on either side. The isolation made Tucker uneasy, but anywhere this transaction were to take place would have made him uneasy.

Calvin took it slow down the unpaved driveway, careful not to ride the Firebird's shocks too hard. Dust kicked up and swirled in through the open T-top. Tucker covered his mouth to keep out most of the dirt which, this being an Iowa farm, he assumed was fifty percent manure.

The fields were low, as if nothing was planted on them at all. The telltale smells of livestock were absent. Whoever lived on this acreage made their money some way other than farming.

The sky had gone overcast in thick gray clouds like lint balls overhead. A slow breeze moved a tire swing on the oak in front of the farmhouse. The house itself was well kept. White with dark green shutters. Trimmed lawn. No rusting farm implements in the yard like most properties in the Midwest.

"Should I be scared?" Tucker asked.

"Every day, all the time," Calvin said. "That way you don't get surprised and you don't get hurt."

Calvin turned off the car, reached over Tucker's lap and opened the glove box to remove a .38.

Seeing Tucker's reaction Calvin said, "Relax. This is a just-in-case gun. This ain't enough to get in any real trouble."

"I'm not all that interested in any trouble, real or imagined."

Tucker stared down his grandson. "You sure your mom didn't fuck the milkman?" Calvin popped his door open, slid the .38 into the belt on his pants and walked toward the door. Tucker chased after him, a feeling in his chest like a rope tightening around his heart.

Before Calvin reached the top step on the porch the door opened. A man stood just inside, a shadow cutting him at the knees and making his face impossible to see. A long straight shape ran down from the man's right arm. Tucker thought it could either be an umbrella or a shotgun. He made up the part about the umbrella to make himself feel better.

"Help you?" said the shadow.

"I hope so," started Calvin. "You owe my son, Webb McGraw."

"Maybe I know him."

"Oh, no, I know you know him. I said you owe him. About five grand as I heard it. We're gonna need that."

Tucker inadvertently shielded his body with Calvin's. When he realized he was doing it he felt ashamed to be hiding behind an 86-year-old man.

"You're his dad, you said?"

"And this here's his son." Tucker held up a hand in a short wave. "This is not a shakedown. You owe that money legit. I aim to collect it. Seems my son is in a bit of trouble. We're gonna need some resources to help him out."

The shadow stepped forward into the flat cloud-covered light. The man wore a T-shirt, dirty jeans. Long drooping mustache, silver hoop earrings in both ears, tan skin that pegged him as at least part Latino. You could practically hear the rumble of a Harley between his legs. He did not hold an umbrella.

"What's wrong with Webb?" the man said with genuine concern.

Calvin kept on speaking in his even keel. No need to relax because he'd been relaxed from the get-go. Tucker felt the rope around his heart slacken a bit.

"Seems he got in a bit of a mess with the Stanleys."

"No shit?"

"None at all. Ambrose, is it?"

"Call me Brose." Ambrose lifted his chin, his form of a handshake. Calvin reciprocated. Ambrose scratched the soul patch below his lip, smoothed his mustache with his forefinger and thumb. "Wish I could help you man. I don't got it right now. Webb was giving me a few more weeks."

"I don't have weeks, Brose."

"I don't got it. Sorry, man."

"You have a son, Brose?" Calvin was all faux friendliness.

"No, man. I don't."

"But, you have something that's valuable to you."

The tip of the shotgun lifted very slightly. Like an animal smelling a threat from across a valley, Ambrose tightened his senses.

When he didn't answer, Calvin continued. "The other accessory we're gonna need for this trouble we're in is another ride."

"You got a pretty sweet set of wheels right there, bro."

"Yeah, but see, I don't want anything to happen to that. If Webb is my son, that there is my baby girl. So we need another vehicle."

"Can't help you, man. I got a pickup but it's got a hundred fifty thousand on it, tailgate's busted off, stereo don't work."

"I knew your name, Brose. I knew where you lived. What makes you think I wouldn't know about your car?"

Calvin stepped off the porch, turned left and began walking toward the barn. Tucker chased after him, suddenly exposed and aware of how close the shotgun was. Deep tire ruts finished the path from the driveway to the double barn doors and Calvin walked steadily to the classic American red-painted barn.

Ambrose followed anxiously. "Why you want my car, man?"

"I told you. We need it or the five grand."

"I don't have the cash, man."

"Then it's settled."

Calvin opened the barn doors. Tucker waited for the shotgun to erupt.

There was only silence. Silence and a bright orange 1970 Plymouth Superbird, a car most notable for the absolutely ridiculous three-foot-high spoiler on the back. A genuine stock car, made street legal and sold to hicks, rednecks and outlaws for a few short years before even GM realized how silly it was.

To Calvin, she was a centerfold beckoning him forward with a smoldering look and whispering, "Turn-ons: guys who drive fast, white hair, senior discounts and arthritis." It was automotive Viagra.

"Come on, man," Ambrose said, appealing to the better part of Calvin's manhood.

"Nothing personal, Brose. Just business. Keys?"

Tucker looked at the pumpkin-colored eyesore and knew this was what his dad wanted him to have posters of in his room growing up. Not Joe Montana and Troy Aikman. Cars like this, cars in general, were where the communication began to break down.

"I can't let you take my car, man."

Tucker snapped out of his memory. Here came the shotgun shells. No help for miles. In Iowa, no one could hear you scream.

"I'll bring it back. And know this, Brose. No one respects a vehicle more than me. Look at my baby. Cherry as the day she was born. I know what you got here. She's a classic. Proud as a peacock. Think of it as a rental. I'll drive it five grand worth and then bring it back."

Ambrose worked his soul patch some more. Almost wore his lip clean. The shotgun weighed in his hand. Tucker could see him feeling its weight versus the weight of killing two men. Over a car.

"Let me make it easy on you," Calvin said. He swooped up a hand, gripped the barrel of the shotgun and twisted it, ripping it free from the younger man's grasp. Once Calvin held the single barrel firmly he pushed forward, driving the butt of the gun into Ambrose's chest, knocking the wind out of him.

Tucker backed up until he hit the side of the Superbird. He turned his head, saw the spoiler almost at eye level and flinched, thinking it was someone else in the room.

Ambrose stumbled back, hit hard off a post from one of the old horse stables and fell to the dirt and straw floor. Calvin followed him and swung the stock of the gun like a golf club, clipping the man's chin and making a sound like a backfire in the high-ceilinged barn.

Calvin stood over him, Tucker held his breath. Ambrose groaned from the ground.

"Keys," demanded Calvin. Ambrose dug into his front pocket. Two small keys on a single ring. "Can't say I didn't give you a chance, kid."

Calvin spun and tossed the keys to Tucker. He flinched again and cringed like a flaming sack of shit was headed his way. The keys hit him in the chest and fell to the ground.

"Ow," he said.

"You drive that one," Calvin said.

"Me? Why?"

"Because no one but me drives the Bandit."

Calvin turned and walked out of the barn back toward his car, taking the shotgun with him. Tucker almost stepped over to check on Ambrose, but thought twice. The faster he was off the farm, the better.

He feared Ambrose's retaliation. After all, how you gonna keep 'em down on the farm after you'd kicked their ass? For the time being, though, it was Calvin's problem.

The acoustics in the barn turned out to be perfect for the throaty roar of the Superbird's engine.

Deep down in Tucker, in a place that didn't have a name, something stirred. An echo through the ages, a flash of lightning down the helix of his DNA .

Tucker barely noticed, but above, the clouds parted a little, carving a path of light for the drive home.

7

With the Trans Am safely stored away in Tucker's garage Calvin powered the Superbird and its ridiculous tailfeather toward the office of Hugh Stanley.

"You mind telling me what we gain by doing this?" Tucker asked.

Calvin drove with one arm propped in the open window, breeze blowing his still-thick hair. "You dealt with one of the kids, right?"

"Kenny."

"Yeah. You'll never find out anything that way. We go to the top. Lucky for you, we have an in. Me. Hugh Stanley will see me and he'll act glad as hell. Inside he'll be shitting a brick, and if he is, that will tell me a hell of a lot about what really happened to Webb."

"You think the Stanleys are behind it?"

"I doubt it. They'd be pretty stupid to take out one of their best men. But, it's a start. Our other option is to start knocking on doors and asking if anyone has seen him. Or take out one of those milk carton ads."

Tucker folded his hands in his lap, squeezed until his

knuckles turned white. "If it's not the Stanleys then who?"

"No idea. First thing is to find out what he was hauling. You neglected to get that little tidbit when Kenny came to see you."

"He wouldn't say."

"Right. Uh-huh. If we know what it was we might know who else wanted it. Highest rate of trouble for a driver is a jacking. By nature we always have valuables on board. Lots of big-for-their-britches types like to try to cut in on some of that. All reward and no risk. At least they think no risk. In my experience, you jack a driver—a good, connected one—you always come out the loser."

"Did you ever get hijacked?"

"Sure. Lots of times."

"And they never got away with it?"

"Not once. Most of 'em never even got a look at the goods."

Tucker turned to his grandfather. "So, wait, that means you..."

"I did my job, kid. Deliver the goods. That's what I'm paid for."

"Were paid for."

"Yeah." A dim mask came over Calvin's face. The kind of melancholy usually reserved for thoughts of a lost loved one. For Calvin, it was the loss of his greatest love— the job.

His wife said goodbye. In the hospital, attached to those machines. The moments were few and getting fewer that she could communicate through the fog of drugs and the tubes down her throat, up her nose. The worst was the hole they drilled in her skull. An electric wire ran from beneath the bone to a small screen that pulsed with tangled yarn lines and beeped like an alarm clock with no snooze button.

They were alone. She gripped his hand and he opened his eyes, sleep wasn't coming anyhow. She said her goodbyes. She knew. He knew. They kissed, a rubber hose marring an otherwise perfect meeting of lips. So familiar it took him back to a time before the alcohol smell and the bedpans. Back to a time when he would come home from a run and sweep her up in his arms, still fueled with adrenaline, and race her to bed to make love.

Even now any electronic beep made him think of that kiss. The machine's little robot mosquitos in his ear as he tried to have a last peaceful moment with his wife.

"Turn it off," she said to him.

He clicked a switch and the room fell in to wonderful silence. Backseat in a clear-cut cornfield staring at the stars kind of silence. He held her, gripped her strong so she would be sure to feel it. She inhaled his aftershave, burying her nose between his neck and his shirt collar. The smell of him. The smell of a life lived in love.

They had their twenty seconds of farewell before two nurses and a doctor rushed in to save her, the machine suddenly showing no signs of brain function at all.

The silence burst apart, the smell faded from her senses but the memory remained. Calvin was banned from being in her room unsupervised. He stayed away for three days. He woke up on day four and knew it was pointless to go in. The call came a half hour later.

But they'd said goodbye.

The job ended before he could give it one last farewell. The calls stopped coming. Too old. Too risky. Nothing to do but move to Omaha. If death had a waiting room, that was it.

Behind the wheel of the Plymouth, Calvin savored his last kiss.

***

"Calvin you old rumrunner, how the hell have you been?" Hugh Stanley stood, as sure a sign of respect as you were to get out of the old man.

Tucker hung back a courteous three paces as Calvin entered the office.

"Hugh. Been a long time."

"A long time. Good grief. I suppose you're here about Webb." Not ones for chit chat, the Stanley men.

The headquarters of the Stanley family empire of crime were housed in a three story office complex that still had the outlines from the long-gone letters of an aluminum siding company that used to own the place. Hugh had overseen the purchase of the building back in the late 80s as a way to appear legitimate. Hugh and the extended family occupied the bottom floor of suites and the top two sat vacant. A sign on the building advertised space for rent, but any time someone actually called the number they were told the space had just been rented that morning.

The carpet needed changing back in the Clinton years and the lighting was nothing but fluorescent tubes in the ceiling so every room had floor lamps and desk lamps pooling light in a permanent indoor dusk.

Hugh padded over the fake oriental rug he'd spread over the ruined carpet. Two leather chairs sat facing Hugh's important-looking desk. Hugh sat back down without offering a seat to his guests.

"Wish I had some news for you. Truth be told, I was kinda hoping you boys would have an easier time raising some word from him. A call from the road. A postcard."

"From the islands, perhaps?"

"I hope he didn't try to drive my truck to an island. We'll be pulling him out of the bottom of the ocean."

Calvin stood, waiting to be offered a chair. Old fashioned manners. "You had him on a truck job?"

"Yes, sir. Big payday too. I don't see why he chose to take off with the goods. It was a fair price for an easy run."

A mutual distrust ran between the two men, Tucker could sense it. They spoke with the veiled acrimony usually reserved for family members.

"And what, to you, is a fair price?"

Hugh laughed. "Let's not get into money now, shall we?"

"I'd like to know."

"It makes no difference. It was more than fair. A three hour pizza job. One way delivery."

"If you're asking ten million from my grandson here," Calvin gestured to Tucker who shrank under the attention. "What is a fair percentage of that amount?"

"That number could be a lot higher if we weren't talking about a McGraw."

Calvin took a seat. Breaking protocol his way of telling Hugh the master and servant relationship had changed. The gesture fit with Calvin's general fuck-you-I'm-old mentality. Standing on ceremony was a young man's game, and with that, Tucker stayed standing.

"Look, Hugh, your dad and my dad, you and me, your sons and my son, your grandsons and..." Calvin stopped himself from gesturing to Tucker again. "We've got a lot of history.

You want Webb found, so do I. More so. I need something more. What was he hauling? Let's start there."

Hugh let it be known with a long sigh and a folding of his hands that he didn't appreciate the tone, but he explained anyway. Tucker felt weak in the knees.

"And it was an eighteen-wheeler you say?"

"Direct from the plant where they make the stuff."

"Webb didn't do big rigs."

"Said he did."

Calvin scratched his chin. He hadn't shaved that morning and the sound of his stubble being scraped filled the silence. The sound of a man gathering clues.

"You'd think something that big would be hard to hide," Calvin said.

"You'd think," Hugh said. "But we hid one for him to pick up."

"True, true." Calvin went back to working his scratch. Hugh let the man stew, watched him with a finger on his chin like he was trying to read his thoughts.

"Y'know what, Cal? I have an idea." Hugh leaned forward on his desk, interlaced his fingers out in front of him. "More of a proposal, if you will."

Calvin raised his eyebrows, a gesture that said, I'm listening.

Tucker looked on, happy to be ignored in the room and wondering what about his fate was about to be decided.

"You still seem on top of your game. Got your grandson here to help you. And McGraws and Stanleys go together like gasoline and spark plugs, right? And like you said, you want to find Webb and I want to find him."

Calvin nodded once, acknowledging the truth in his statement.

45

"We still owe delivery of payment to the two punks who jacked the truck in the first place. It was supposed to be payment on delivery, which we never got, but we have every evidence that Webb was there. Even left a stolen car for them to keep. A payoff like this, when I got no product at the end of the deal, is one reason why this whole deal sours my stomach, but Stanleys are no welchers. Anyway, what I'm driving at, I bet you have a lot of questions for those boys. Why don't you make the delivery for me? Drive out there, give them their cash and then you do whatever the hell you want. Ask 'em questions, take 'em to dinner, give 'em a bath I don't care. What do you say?"

"Me drive for you again?" A grin curled the edges of Calvin's mouth.

"Let's go one further, come work for me. Take that debt and work it off. I'm no fool, I know you don't have that kind of money. We just wanted to see if we could beat the bushes a little, scare Webb out of hiding."

"If I knew where he was hiding, Hugh, I'd do the beating myself."

Hugh laughed again, the patronizing laugh of a supervisor inviting his subordinate into the parlor to talk like equals, knowing the equality ended on the other side of the door.

"I know you would, Cal, I know you would. What do you say? Want to fire up the old pistons again? My operation isn't right without a McGraw on the payroll. Like we got a flat tire around here."

"You can cool it with the car talk. I get your point. And we'll take it."

If Tucker had been offered a drink he would have spit it. His neck cracked when his head whipped so fast to the left.

Calvin ignored the slack-jawed stare and stood.

"I recently got me a new ride and I've been eager to try it out."

"You got rid of the Bandit?"

"Oh, no. But she's more like the fine china. Only comes out on special occasions."

Calvin offered his hand across the desk and Hugh stood to shake it. Calvin beckoned Tucker over to do the same.

"Great to have you aboard, boys. We'll put our heads together about this Webb thing and in the meantime, you can drive off what he stole."

"Allegedly," Calvin corrected. He stopped pumping his hand but held Hugh's palm firm, looked him straight in the eye.

"Yes, counselor," Hugh said with a smile. "Now, it's gonna take me a day or two to put together the payoff. You sit back and I'll give you a call when it's ready to go. We'll be in touch."

In the circular driveway the bright orange car stood out among the black BMWs and Mercedes like a pimple on a prom date.

"What the hell was that all about?" Tucker's voice nearly cracked.

"We got ourselves a job."

"I know that. Driving for Stanley? I told you I'm not a criminal."

"No, but you are a McGraw. And we stick together. We can learn a hell of a lot more about what happened to Webb from the inside. Don't you want to talk to those Illinois boys? I know I do. Or did you want to go back to my knocking on doors idea? Or I can go home and you can raise the ten million on your own."

Tucker sputtered like an out of sync gearbox. "Yeah, but, I don't know how to do all that... driving stuff."

"You got me. Don't worry. You'll be like my apprentice." Calvin opened the door and slid behind the wheel. Tucker followed into the passenger seat.

"It seems dangerous to get this close to the Stanleys before we know what they had to do with it. I mean, a truckload full of drugs? Who knows what these guys are capable of?"

"First, it was truckload of stuff to make drugs with. Second, I know what they're capable of. They're capable of killing both of us and feeding our severed body parts to pigs on a dozen different farms across the tri-county area. And if they wanted to do that, we'd already be in different trucks headed east." Tucker swallowed hard. "You ever hear the expression keep your friends close but your enemies closer?"

"That's what we're doing?"

"Nope. I think that's what they're doing."

The Superbird engine growled to life.

8

"You think they're afraid of us?" Tucker asked as he handed Calvin a second beer. Calvin's calloused finger lifted, pushed and folded back the tab. The old man missed the days when you'd lift that tab right off. Then some dumbass in Connecticut went and choked on one of those little metal deals and we got safety cans.

Calvin leaned a hip against the counter in the kitchen. Webb's house was cold, but the fridge was well-stocked in beer. Like father, like son, unlike grandson.

"I'm just sayin' what better way to keep eyes on us than to bring us into the fold. They'll know if we get close to finding Webb and then, if there's something they don't want us to know," Calvin raised an eyebrow, hinting that he felt this was a very strong option, "they can throw us off the scent."

"Okay, I guess." Tucker sipped on his own beer, using his slow nursing drinking style that drove real drinkers crazy. "Won't that make it harder for us to find out anything?"

"Not if we know they don't want us to know things. If we know they're trying to stop us, they can't stop us. We'll be one step ahead."

What he wasn't saying, what Tucker should have been able to tell, was that Calvin almost jumped for joy at being back in the game. Like a pitcher who got called up from the minors for one last game, Calvin was going to make the best of it and savor every detail.

The ink had faded but the indent of the writing still cut deep into the layers of paint. TUCKER AGE 13 and a line, about chest height to Tucker now. When they came to Webb's house Tucker had forgotten how long it had been since he'd been inside his childhood home.

Now that the fridge had been raided of beer he and Calvin could begin their search for clues. Not that Webb left much in the way of paperwork or anything connected to his job. Calvin already knew more than they could learn spending a week inside the tired-looking home, and that was from speaking to his son on the phone from a state away at least once a week.

Tucker wandered around the familiar rooms not touching anything. He felt like he was touring a section of his own brain, a part that kept memories of his childhood. To touch something would open a rift in time and space and he might be sucked in, taken back to the 1980s. No one wanted that.

Calvin stepped deeper into the house than Tucker was willing to go so he waited in the living room, seeing ghosts of his mother fluffing pillows. The McGraw women—silent sufferers of the life the men couldn't leave behind. Maybe that's why Jenny left. She saw the writing on the wall. Plain as the height chart carved into the kitchen doorway, a line marking out each year closer to the end.

Calvin came back inside from the garage, his second beer can empty. "Hmmm."

"What?"

"His cars are all here. Don't seem like Webb to split without one of his babies."

Three of them out there, all classic American muscle. All had girls names, the sisters Tucker never had.

"They said he left in a semi-truck."

"And I said he didn't drive any semi. Not unless he snuck out and took a course without me knowing. Seems odd he would hide that from me. The boy told me when he took a crap that clogged the john. Why would he hide work-related stuff from me?"

Tucker shook his head. If he wasted words every time he didn't know the answers behind his dad's actions, his throat would be raw.

Just as Calvin was screwing his face into a thinking scowl the cell phone in his pocket rang a digital version of an old time phone bell. He didn't seem to notice, lost in thought as he looked at nothing in the living room.

Tucker waited for him to answer. Two rings. Three.

"Granddad?"

"Huh?"

"Your phone."

He came to, took the phone from his pocket and flipped it open. "Yeah?"

Tucker watched him nod like he was taking instructions.

"No problem." He hung up, turned to Tucker. "Got our first job."

"Guess we're going across the river."

"Not yet."

"What?"

Calvin pocketed his phone. He explained to Tucker what

he'd heard on the phone. The studied look on his face read to Tucker like he was parsing the full meaning of the conversation as he talked.

"Money won't be ready until tomorrow. They're sending us on a back and forth until then."

"What does that mean?"

"Just what it sounds like. Take something somewhere and bring it back."

Tucker studied Calvin. "You don't look too sure."

"Oh it's a back and forth all right. I kinda figure it might be something more though. Must be some reason it can't wait. Unless they're just excited to have cheap labor."

"What do we do? Do we go?"

"Yep. We go and we watch our asses." Calvin pulled the Superbird keys from his pocket and spun them around his finger, turned for the door and led Tucker out.

If he'd been standing anywhere else Tucker would have hesitated, protested the wisdom of the whole plan. Being in the haunted house of his youth he made for the door almost as fast as he had when he was eighteen, suitcase in hand and registration forms for community college in his back pocket.

The job was a transport. The cargo was human.

Calvin instructed Tucker to remain silent, let the old pro handle the finesse required for a job of this pedigree. His exact words were, "Shut up. Don't say or do a fucking thing and whatever happens, do NOT interact with him. He's as inanimate as a bag of hammers as far as you're concerned."

Calvin pulled the Superbird to a stop in front of the last room on the bottom row of a motel and let the car idle. He cracked his neck in a fast twisting motion that looked painful to Tucker.

After three minutes listening to the music of the V-8 sipping slowly at the gasoline, a man emerged.

Calvin nodded and Tucker got out, flipped his seat forward so the man could climb in back.

Their cargo was young, mid-twenties. Vintage leather jacket, jeans a few weeks between washes and a sunglasses resting on a bed of short spiked hair above his forehead.

"You guys my limousine?"

Tucker showed him the open door, his brain humming, "Don't talk to him. Don't talk to him. Bag of hammers. Bag of hammers."

The man took in the full view of the bright orange Plymouth. "What the fuck is this?"

Calvin had no such rule about not talking to the cargo. "It's a classic. Get in."

The man folded himself into the back seat and Tucker took his place in front.

"You know where we're going?" the man asked.

"Yep," Calvin said.

"Okay. Name's Richie. Looks like we're gonna be in business together, eh?"

"I'm only here to drive you. Whatever business you got is yours alone."

Calvin dropped the car in gear and roared off.

It was a thirty minute drive to the lake. Richie tried several times to make conversation, his nervous energy getting the best of him. From what Tucker could discern, they were driving Richie to some sort of meeting with the Stanleys, which ones he wasn't sure.

"You boys think maybe you ought to use a less... um,

conspicuous car next time?"

Calvin kept his arm planted in the window, working hard on his trucker's tan. "Car like this is meant to be driven. Nice jaunt to the lake is exactly what a machine like this needs."

Richie tapped out a beat on his knees. Tucker could sense he wanted so badly to have someone else to look at and comment, "You believe this fucking guy?"

Tucker answered in his head. "No. No, I don't at all."

The cabin stood lakeside with a small dock jutting out into the flat water. Bass fishing country. A simple fiberglass boat with an Evinrude clamped to the back sat tied to the crooked wooden dock.

Standing in the doorway were three men, all in plaid flannel shirts and Timberlands.

Calvin parked, Tucker got out and repeated the flipping forward of the seat. Richie stood straight, clapped his hands together and went into business mode. "Gentlemen!"

The three men escorted Richie inside. Tucker thought he recognized one of them as Kenny Stanley.

Calvin got out and leaned against the door, folded his arms and looked to Tucker indicating he should do the same. Calvin still hadn't indicated how long this meeting might take, but by his body language Tucker assumed they would be there for a while.

"What now?" Tucker asked in a whisper.

"We wait."

"How long?"

"Don't know. However long it takes them to discuss their business."

"They didn't tell you on the phone?"

"All they said was bring him here and wait until it's done. That's all I need to know. Whatever they're talking about in there ain't my business. Or yours."

Calvin turned toward the lake. Tucker slapped at a mosquito trying to find purchase on his neck.

There were sounds from inside. Sounded to Tucker like someone dumped a bag of apples on the wood floors. Then a "Hey!".

Tucker turned to Calvin who kept his gaze on the water.

The back door opened and Richie came out being helped along by the three Stanley men. Richie's hands were bound with heavy chains. A flannel-shirted man had each arm and the third followed with a sack that was obviously very heavy. The man looked as if he could lift almost anything with no trouble but he strained at the burlap sack.

Tucker unfolded his arms and straightened. Calvin quietly put out a hand to keep him in place. "Steady."

"Yeah, but—"

"I know."

The quartet headed for the dock. Richie's muffled screams were muted by the red handkerchief in his mouth, the ball of red spilling out like a blood clot.

Richie's body went limp, an old trick, but his two escorts held him up as his toes dragged through the wet leaves on the ground. The work boots of the Stanley men pounded on the weathered boards of the dock and two ducks took flight at the sound. Tucker could hear the chains rattle around Richie's wrists.

He came around the front of the car to Calvin's side.

"Aren't we going to stop them?" he whispered.

Calvin took his eyes off the lake and bore them into Tucker.

"No."

Tucker turned back to the lake as the men reached the small craft. Richie's protestations nearly capsized them as the two men wrestled him to the bottom of the boat. The man carrying the heavy sack set it in the back and took hold of the rope and pulled the tiny engine to life.

As they puttered away Tucker felt he knew the feeling of watching a man walk to the gallows. The boat's wake splashed over the dock and darkening the wood slats.

The water returned to calm. The motor sound faded as the boat receded further toward the center of the lake. The two ducks returned to float beside the dock as if the threat had passed. It had, thought Tucker, but not for Richie.

Tucker turned to Calvin who looked away from the lake now. His face was solid as the tree bark surrounding them. Tucker stared hard, waiting for an explanation.

"It's a test," Calvin said. "They want us to know they're serious."

"What do we do?"

"We sit here and take it. We let them know we don't spook easy."

"But that guy, Richie—"

"He was gonna get it anyway. You don't know him, what he did. You shouldn't even know his name. Forget it."

Tucker turned back to the lake to see a shape go overboard. The sound took a moment to reach the shore. Soon after the boat began powering back to the dock. When it landed, only three men got out.

They all entered the house by the back door they'd come out with Richie. The heavy sack was gone.

Kenny came out of the front and stood on the porch. He

addressed Calvin.

"All done here. You can go."

Calvin didn't say a word, turned to the car and gave Tucker a look that said, follow my lead and shut up. He obeyed and got in the car.

Calvin got back behind the wheel, cranked the engine to life. Tucker saw the two ducks take off again to circle the lake one more time. He knew after the rumble of the engine had gone they would return; the threat over. Calm, flat water again.

Tucker read with interest one time about the world record for holding your breath. Over seven minutes. The article said most people couldn't go more than two.

As they retraced the drive through the woods, Tucker counted.

9

Back at Tucker's house they separated, Tucker putting as much distance between he and Calvin as the generations that divided them.

Alone in his bedroom, Tucker could hear the thin aluminum crack of another Pabst opening in the kitchen.

He'd spent his whole life avoiding not only his father's chosen career, but his entire family lineage. Never before had he come so close to the truth of what McGraw men did for a living. He'd lived through the hypothetical. His sojourn to the lake was an exercise right out of a junior college ethics class. Had he been implicit in Richie's death simply for delivering him to the men who would ultimately do the deed? Was he bound by morality to intervene? Was accessory to murder not just murder under another name?

And the drugs his father was delivering, wasn't he only one step away from putting the crystal in some kid's pipe?

Tucker was broken out of his moral conundrum by a knock at the door. His heart sped up. Opening his front door hadn't brought good news in a few days.

By the time Tucker got out to the living room Calvin already had the door open and was pulling in the figure standing there.

"Come here, you old polecat. Put 'er in the old vice."

He gripped hard on Milo's hand and Tucker saw his son wince a little at Calvin's grasp. Milo had to drop a soft-sided overnight bag in order to take Calvin's handshake. Tucker knew the door wasn't ready to give up any good news yet.

"I'll be a son of a bitch, ain't you big now?"

"Sixteen years old."

"Sixteen you say? The age a McGraw man really comes into it. Get you a driver's license so you don't have to go catting around on the back roads anymore, right?"

"I haven't taken my test yet."

"Well, shit boy. What's the holdup?"

Milo looked over Calvin's shoulder to Tucker who stood in the doorway. Calvin turned and it made sudden sense.

"Is that true, Tuck? The boy doesn't have his license yet?"

"Not yet, Granddad. I don't have a whole lot of time with him these days to take him down there."

"Well, shit boy, the young man needs his wheels. You put a sock around his dick and tie his hands above his waist too?"

Both Tucker and his son blushed. Tucker stepped forward, picked up the bag.

"What's this?"

"I was hoping I could stay with you for a while."

"Milo, we talked about this."

"I know, but..." He turned his eyes down to the worn and dirty mat in the entryway, "she's a bitch sometimes, Dad."

"Milo!"

"I said sometimes."

Calvin broke out in a grin. "Well, don't stand in the doorway boy. Come on in. No bitches in here."

"God, Granddad!" Tucker scolded.

Calvin raised his hands in mock surrender. "Guess I can't offer him a beer then?"

Milo sat on the couch as Tucker closed the door, still holding the bag of clothes his son brought.

"Milo, you know I want nothing more than to have you here with me." Tucker set the bag down next to the couch. "But this doesn't look good to your mother. This could set us back. She's gonna fly off the handle and say I'm turning you against her and all that crap. We just talked about getting more visitation, possibly."

Milo slumped into the couch, exhausted from his parent's years-long fight.

"Just for a few days." The words came out weak, like they were written on thin paper.

"Of course you can," Calvin said.

"It's not up to you," Tucker said.

"No. It's up to the boy. He can decide where he wants to lay his head."

"No, he can't actually. Not until he's eighteen. I know because I've had a judge tell me so." Tucker leveled his gaze at Milo's downturned head. "And he knows it."

"Bullshit."

"Granddad, a driver's license isn't a free pass to do whatever you want, okay? Sixteen is still a child."

"Aw Christ, Tucker. Why don't you cut off the kid's balls while you're at it? Give him a little credit."

Tucker hated giving speeches like this. He wanted to build memories Milo would want to relive, not run from. He let out a deep sigh, challenging Milo for the most exhausted and resigned McGraw in the room.

"Does your mom know where you are?"

Milo looked up. "No. My buddy Derek dropped me off."

Calvin brushed past Tucker on his way to the kitchen. Under his breath he said, "That kid has his license."

Tucker ignored him. "Let's go call her." Milo dropped his head again. "To tell her you'll be here for a few days."

Milo perked up.

Three sounds stacked one on top of the other: Milo's sigh of relief, the crack and hiss of another beer can opening from the kitchen and a fist rattling the door.

Tucker turned to the rattling. He began to hate even having an entrance to the house. He thought of barricading the door the way he would in a zombie movie.

Calvin rushed in from the kitchen, the beer foaming over his palm.

"Open up motherfucker!"

The voice sounded vaguely familiar. If it were Stanley's men the door would be open and shots would have been fired already.

"Gimme my fucking car back, bitch!"

Tucker turned to Calvin. They silently reached the same conclusion. Ambrose.

"It's open!" Calvin said. Tucker's eyes went wide.

After Milo came in no one had locked the door. Better than getting it kicked in, Calvin figured.

The door swung open and Ambrose stood flanked by three men all with the same heavy eyebrows and thick necks. Brothers. Each man held a stick of some sort. A baseball bat, cut off broom handle and a sawed off hockey stick. Not exactly a posse with guns blazing but enough for a room with an octogenarian, an insurance salesman and an unlicensed teenager.

"You here with our money?" asked Calvin, his bravado faking it in place of a plan.

"You ain't gonna get the jump on me now, motherfucker."

Milo brought his feet up on the couch, curled into a ball worried that he was in some sort of scared straight program to keep him from running out on Jenny.

Tucker froze in place, wanting very badly to tell Calvin, "Told you so."

"I thought we had a deal, Brose." Calvin said, still the picture of calm.

"The deal now is you give me my goddamn car back, bitch."

"What about my money?"

"Man, shut the fuck up! Can't you see what I'm bringing?" Ambrose gestured to the three mute brothers surrounding him. By their flat-footed stance and the bark-but-no-bite rhetoric so far, Calvin knew these boys were nothing to fear. Still, uninvited house guests could be hard to get rid of sometimes.

"Relax, Brose. You want a beer? I'll get you gentlemen a beer." Calvin stepped back into the kitchen. Ambrose tensed, seeing his control of the situation eroding. Tucker stayed glued to the carpet.

"Get back here, motherfucker, and give me my keys."

Calvin reappeared with a fresh beer can in each hand. "Afraid all I have is two left. I guess I've been hitting it a little harder than I thought." He smiled and then hurled the can in his right hand in a fast pitch at Ambrose, then switched the other can to his right hand and reeled back for another pitch.

Tucker bobbed his head back as the can of Pabst sailed

past him at an impressive speed. Ambrose wasn't the bobber Tucker was and took a 12 oz can to the bridge of his nose.

The three brothers blinked like a family of possums caught on a highway at night. Calvin chose the thick-necked brothers on the right for the second can and caught him a ricochet shot across the temple.

"Let's go!" Calvin shouted to his grandsons.

Milo scrambled fast up and over the couch and Tucker ran by instinct to the sound of Calvin's voice.

"To the garage," Calvin instructed. The trio shot down the hallway.

The remaining brothers stopped to help their fallen comrades then took two hesitant steps to follow their prey, stopped to stay, shuffled forward but couldn't advance like their kin were magnets holding them close.

"Get those fuckers!" Ambrose said through the bloodstained hands he held over his nose.

Calvin threw open the door to the garage and without looking launched himself forward, missing the three steps down. He pitched forward and hit hard on the passenger door of the Plymouth, grunting out a made-up curse word, "Fuckapuss-cock!"

Tucker stepped up behind him and put a hand under his armpit. "Get him in," he said to Milo.

Tucker stood Calvin upright and dug a hand into his granddad's pocket pulling the single key ring out as Milo opened the door and pushed his great grandfather into the back seat. Tucker moved around the front end of the Road Runner, fumbling with the keys and thinking again about the zombie movie and how this would be the exact moment the engine didn't start.

He slid into the driver's seat and the engine turned over no problem.

As Ambrose and his three cousins came piling out of the front door, the two healthy men helping along the two injured, the rumble of the Superbird's V-8 already spilled out from the garage.

The tires squealed on the slick garage floor surface and the rubber smoked before catching grip and blasting the car out of the garage. Tucker hit the street with no idea where to turn. Instinct took over. Fear drove the car, not Tucker, but from the backseat Calvin felt he was witnessing a rebirth.

"That's it, boy. Drive it like you stole it!" he said.

"We did steal it!" Tucker said, his eyes wild and trying to see every possible obstacle in his way at once.

Milo was shocked into silence at seeing his father behind the wheel of a strange, loud car doing anything over 35 miles an hour.

Tucker reached the stop sign at the end of his block, screeched the tires again to make his stop before the white line.

"Fuck the stop signs, kid."

Tucker knew he was right. He regrouped, inhaled deep and spun a U-turn.

"Where the hell are you going?" Calvin asked.

"This way is better," Tucker said.

He drove back past his own house as the pickup truck with Ambrose and his cousins banged away from the curb.

Tucker felt thankful for the automatic gearbox on the Superbird. Shifting would be one thing too many to worry about. He powered the car through the suburban streets as fast as he could make it.

The pickup had its soundtrack of clangs and rattles. Ambrose hadn't been kidding about the rust and dents exterior, the broken tailgate and the hundred thousand plus milage. He leaned his head back in the passenger seat applying direct pressure to his nose wound while one cousin drove. The two unlucky ones clung for dear life in the open air in back. The sawed off hockey stick bounced twice and flipped out the open tailgate to the street. The owner wasn't about to let go of his two-fisted grip to try to snatch it. It was life over limb in the back of that truck.

Tucker reached the end of his subdivision and turned onto a long straight road that ran along farmland between there and town. The sun was gone on the far horizon and the deep blues of dusk faded to black quickly as the ghosts of bootleggers past came out overhead to usher the McGraw boys along. Some would look up and see stars, but Calvin knew better.

Tucker took the hard left turn too fast. He knew nothing of the car's limits, or any car for that matter. The back end began to fishtail out and Tucker, he wasn't sure why, cranked the wheel and turned into the slide, keeping the car on track and unleashing a wild banshee cry from the tires as they slid along the Iowa asphalt still warm from the faded sunshine.

Calvin nearly teared up. The dormant cells he knew survived inside every McGraw man, even Tucker, were being shocked to life inside the cauldron of fear and high-octane gasoline.

Tucker would never admit to his granddad that he learned that move from Cars. Maybe on Calvin's death bed if he wanted to put the old man out of his misery he could cough up that little detail and it would be enough to send him to the great beyond. Until then, it was between him and the two-lane blacktop.

The pickup skidded onto the country lane losing ground quickly to the Plymouth once they hit the straight. Ambrose punched the dashboard, urging the truck to move faster while simultaneously admiring the well-tuned engine in the Bird. He rarely got to hear the sound from outside the car and it sounded like a big ball of fuck you, like it was supposed to. Made him miss the old gal even more.

The huge wing on the back of the car pushed down on the rear tires and they gripped the road hard like it was a stripper's ass. The pickup faded away in the rearview.

They approached a four-way junction with a single flashing yellow light, the need for traffic control out here unnecessary until that very moment. Tucker slowed, the Bird downshifted and he cut the wheel right to make for town.

When Ambrose saw brake lights he clapped his hands which sent droplets of blood from his soaked hands over the inside of the cab.

"We'll get 'em up here."

In a straight line the pickup still had some guts and they used the braking of the Superbird to gain some ground, but they pushed it a little far. When the pickup finally did brake to make the turn she was coming in hot and the g-force of the right-hand turn sent both cousins in back sailing across the oncoming lane and onto the soft shoulder and the drainage ditch it dipped down into.

The blur of two bodies flying through the air caught in the periphery of the driving cousin and he slowed the truck with a, "Fuck me!"

The two unfortunate siblings landed hard and rolled through fortunately unkempt roadside grass, cushioning their fall and limiting them to a pair of broken legs and more broken ribs than you could count on your fingers.

Tucker revved the Bird back up to eighty before checking the rearview and seeing no headlights following them. He slowed to normal speed and threw a look to Milo whose combination of relief and confusion meant a long explanation he didn't have energy for. He turned to check on Calvin in the cramped backseat and saw a man beaming with pride the way no one did when Tucker graduated from community college. You'd have thought the family had come to witness his first day of life in prison that day.

What Calvin had just witnessed, though, was his coming out party.

"Welcome to the family, Tuck."

10

"What the hell was that, Dad?"

"I was trying to save our lives, that's what." Tucker made sure to lock the door behind him this time. He aimed for the couch and sat hard, dropping his head in his hands.

"Those boys showed up with sticks in their hands, our lives were gonna be fine, " Calvin said. "But, I'll tell you what that was—about damn time. That's what it was. I'm damn proud of you, son. There's a McGraw in there yet."

"It had nothing to do with my name. I was trying to get away from a bunch of madmen who you pissed off. Who's to say they're not headed back here right now?"

"Nah. They learned their lesson. Won't be back for a while. Tell me, did you feel it in your balls?"

"Goddammit." Tucker slumped back into the cushions.

"Tell me if you felt it. I know you did. That feeling never gets old. I still feel it when I go balls out like you just did. Hot damn, I felt like I was eighteen again shootin' the river run racing to get away from smokies with a hot load of contraband in the trunk. Who wants a beer?" Calvin stepped toward the kitchen.

"We're out. You threw them at the men trying to kill us."

Calvin stopped, remembered the last two cans and checked the floor. Both beers had burst when they impacted with Ambrose and his cousins. Each had slowly leaked into the carpet. The wet spot under where Ambrose stood was also colored with some blood.

"Well, crap. We'd better head out to the store then."

Tucker took his hands down from his face. "We're not headed anywhere. Let's get some sleep. I really would like to find my dad and this day has been pissed away by your stupid plans so we're gonna get an early start tomorrow."

The room fell silent until Milo, hands stuffed deep into his jeans and shoulders shrugged up high around his ears, spoke quietly. "Granddad's missing?"

Tucker sighed and palmed his face again. "I told you it wasn't really a good time for you to drop in, Milo. Speaking of, we never called your mom. Let's go do that, otherwise she'll have the cops over here any second."

Tucker stood and Milo followed him into the bedroom to use the phone.

Calvin, still amped from the drive, didn't sit. He stooped and picked up one of the fallen beer cans, shook it, decided there was enough in there to make the effort. He righted himself, spun the can so the tab faced him and cracked the top open with a dull unpressurized aluminum sound. Calvin wiped a smear of blood off the top and tipped the can up to get one decent swig.

Three hours later Tucker picked up the empty pizza box to throw in the trash. He'd tried to entice the other two with one of his frozen pizzas but they insisted on ordering a large with meatball and extra cheese that also came with a two liter Pepsi. Calvin pointed out several times that Pepsi wasn't beer. Tucker told him to deal with it.

"So who gets the couch now?" Calvin asked, eyeing Milo.

"You can have it still. Milo can help me blow up the inflatable. I think I still have your sleeping bag in the closet."

"Aw, man."

"Hey, your choice mister. You keep telling yourself that. Your choices have consequences. For you and for me."

There was no way Milo could adjust his position on the air mattress without making bizarre rubbery noises like two balloon animals humping on a pile of dodgeballs, and the lack of support required constant adjustment.

"Granddad Calvin?" Milo asked, hushed.

"Yeah?" Calvin couldn't get to sleep in silence. Not after getting used to the way Marie snored for all those years.

"Did you and Dad really steal that car?"

Calvin grinned to himself, kept his eyes shut in the darkened room. "What did he tell you?"

"Nothing. He said he'd explain later."

"Well," Calvin turned his body to face the floor where Milo struggled to get comfortable between the TV and the coffee table. "Stealing is in the eye of the beholder. He didn't have what we wanted, so we took what we needed. To me, that's not stealing."

"What did you mean about driving with contraband in the trunk?"

"I shouldn't have said that. Figure of speech. Don't worry about it."

"What about Granddad Webb?"

70

"Oh, he got himself in a bit of trouble. No big deal. We're doing what McGraw men do, though. We got each other's backs. Right?" Calvin opened his eyes and found Milo's profile in the darkened room.

"Yeah."

"That's right we do. Don't you forget it."

11

The phone rang at seven A.M.

Calvin clicked the flip phone shut, turned to Tucker who had been listening from the doorway. "We're going to Illinois."

Milo turned over on his air mattress, loud rubber glove noises filled the room. "What's in Illinois?"

"Not you. You go to school," Calvin said.

"Aw, Dad, come on—"

"He's right," Calvin said. The mischievous granddad had gone. The one that stared down at Milo was dead serious. Milo obeyed.

An hour later they were showered, shaved and Milo had been deposited at school. Calvin accepted the suitcase from the man in the dark suit jacket. He turned and handed it to Tucker to put in the car.

Tucker was shocked by the weight of it. He tried to do some mental calculations to figure how much cash could weigh that much.

Calvin took a piece of paper with their destination on it and he and Stanley's man parted ways without a word. The

Superbird hit I-80 east toward Moline and Rock Island.

Calvin could feel each time Tucker turned his head around to ogle the case in the backseat. It was growing annoying.

"How much do you figure is in there?" Somehow Tucker assumed Calvin would know.

"Don't know, don't care."

"Really?"

"You never look at the cargo. Never open it, never touch it if you don't have to, you don't shake it like a present under a Christmas tree. You never think about it. That's a rule, hard and fast."

Easier said than done. Tucker tried counting lines on the highway but numbers made him think about the case. He tried singing songs in his head but all that came to mind was the Pink Floyd song, Money.

***

It didn't matter how much money was really in the suitcase, from the look of the apartment the two men occupied it was more money than they'd ever seen before.

Calvin carried the case up two flights of stairs. He let Tucker knock. Calvin didn't hide the pistol tucked in his belt.

"Who's there?" The voice inside was paranoid.

"We're from Iowa and we bring good tidings," Calvin said holding up the case for the peephole to see.

"You with the Stanleys?" asked the voice.

"I'm sure they'd appreciate it if you kept that name out of it."

A chain and deadbolt unshackled from inside and the door opened wide. An acrid, chemical smell drooled out of the apartment. The man at the door, thin, chapped lips and nervously pulling on a goatee, stared at the case the way a stray dog looks at a steak.

"That it?"

"We didn't come to Illinois for our health. Can we do this inside?" Calvin said.

The thin man in the Nine Inch Nails T-shirt stepped aside. Calvin entered, Tucker followed.

Sheets hung in all the windows blocking out the sun. The furniture, a couch and two armchairs, looked like it had been found on the street and brought inside. A second man, equally thin and wearing a hooded sweatshirt, took a long last drag on a glass pipe while holding a lighter to the bulb at the end. White smoke swirled around him and he tried to suck it all out of the air and fit more in his lungs like an overstuffed sock drawer.

The smell: explained.

"Pass it over here boys," said the one who answered the door. Neither man had bothered to look Calvin or Tucker in the eyes yet, their focus singular on the case.

"We wanted to ask you boys a few questions about the man who picked up the truck. Is that alright with you, uh... ?"

The one standing finally looked at Calvin, took his expectant face to mean he wasn't getting the case until he introduced himself.

"Randy."

"Randy," Calvin repeated. "And?" He turned to the man on the couch.

"Brent." Brent licked his lips, speeding fast on the last inhale of the pipe double dosed with the anticipation of the contents of that suitcase.

Calvin handed the case to Randy who snatched at it like a hyena after a carcass. He threw the payoff down on the couch next to Brent and fumbled with the clasps.

"So the man who picked up the truck, was he alone?"

Calvin was ignored as the case opened.

Tucker craned his neck around Randy to see. Neat rows of tightly wrapped bills. He still had no idea how much was inside, but he felt a little bit queasy at the thought that he'd been carrying that much.

"Boys?" Calvin said. Nothing. Awestruck. The three wise men weren't so enraptured at a sight as these two tweakers were.

"BOYS?"

Randy turned to Calvin. "Sorry, bro. What?"

He wiped his drippy nose on his hand. Calvin swore he saw tears of joy in the boy's eyes.

"The man who took your cargo, was he alone?"

"No, no man. There were two dudes."

"Did one of them look like us?" Calvin pointed a finger between him and Tucker. Randy was confused.

"No, man. You look like you. They looked like... them."

"I mean, could he have been related?"

Randy looked down at Brent. Brent squinted his eyes. "Could be I guess."

"And they left no problem?"

"Yeah. They checked the load and took off."

"Checked the load? They opened the back of the truck you mean?"

"Yeah. They took a look-see and then hit the road. You guys want to blaze? We got some weed around here too if you want. Got an atomizer." Randy began to search the room from his standing place.

"No, we're okay." Calvin sensed he was losing them. "What can you tell me about the other guy?"

"What other guy?" Brent said.

"The guy who drove the truck." Calvin was growing annoyed. "The one who didn't look like us. Did anyone use his name?"

"No, man," Randy said. He reached out and Brent handed him the glass pipe followed by the lighter. Randy held the pipe up to the light to check the bulb and see how loaded it was.

"Hey, guys. We're still talking here."

Tucker flinched when the lighter sparked. He worried about paranoid things like getting a contact high, the things he'd read about meth labs exploding, the cops busting in. And not so paranoid things like the gun in Calvin's belt.

"Hey," Calvin put a hand on Randy's arm, stopping the pipe from reaching his lips. The lighter burned the air between them.

"What the fuck? What do you want from us, old man? You did your job, now go."

"What I want from you is a little respect for my son." Calvin reached out and pushed Randy's other hand up at the elbow. The lighter flame pressed into his cheek and he screamed. The pipe fell to the floor.

Brent stood up. "Woah!"

Calvin took Randy's shirt in both hands, pulled him in close until the rotten teeth smell filled Calvin's nostrils. "I'm asking you some simple questions here. You'd do well to cooperate."

Tucker watched Brent as he bent to the floor and came up with a bong about three feet long in green glass with a Grateful Dead skull as the bowl. Brent raised the water pipe over his head to use as a club but Tucker stepped forward and kicked at Brent's leg. He caught the back of Brent's knee and heard a pop.

Brent howled and went to the carpet, a place no one should have to endure. Mystery stains, mouse turds, body fluids by the gallon. He grabbed at his knee like a football player after a career ender.

"I don't know anything," Randy said.

"You sure don't. Don't know shit, do you? What did the guy look like?"

"I don't know, man. I don't remember."

"Short, tall, fat, thin?"

"Uh, uh, kinda fat. Medium height. Had a big belt buckle."

"So you still got a few brain cells in there, don't you?"

"That's all I remember. I swear."

Calvin pushed Randy to his knees, stood over him with a firm grip still on the T-shirt. "You gonna remember me? Are you?"

"Yes, sir. I mean, no. Whatever you want."

"Well, the man you can't recall is my son. He's gone missing now with your load. All I wanted was a few simple answers but you're too goddamn busy. Got a suitcase full of cash and now you're a hotshot. Is that it?"

Randy sputtered, his eyes about to come loose from the speed and the crazed old man in his face.

"Next time, you answer someone when they ask you a goddam question."

Calvin let Randy go and he fell to the carpet with his friend. Calvin bent down and picked up the pipe. He stepped one foot over Randy, the boy's shoulders between his feet. With his left hand he grabbed the front of the shirt, with his right he held the pipe.

"Open up." He shook the boy.

Randy tried to focus his eyes, but the room was racing out toward the edge of space at a million miles an hour.

"You want this?" Calvin held up the pipe. "Open."

Randy opened his mouth. Tucker stood back, keeping an eye on Brent who still wailed on the floor. Tucker spotted Randy's shirt ride up exposing a glimpse of white belly. He turned his eyes away.

Calvin pushed the glass pipe into Randy's mouth. Didn't stop at his lips. Pushed it and kept going. Nearly fit the whole thing in until only the blackened bulb sat outside his lips like a spit bubble waiting to pop. Randy gagged with deep retching sounds.

Calvin let go of the shirt and moved his hand under Randy's chin and pushed his mouth shut. The glass crunched. He pulled the jaw open and the broken bulb fell into the opening. Calvin pushed on the chin again and the glass bulb popped inside like a ripe grape.

Working Randy's mouth like a nurse feeding an invalid, Calvin pumped his chin up and down crushing the glass inside. Stifled screams tried to escape Randy's mouth.

Tucker stepped forward and put a hand on his granddad's shoulder.

"Stop it. Stop."

Calvin stood abruptly, breathing heavy, his face red with hot blood just under the surface.

"Next time you answer a man when he talks to you."

Randy rolled over and coughed out a slime of crushed glass, saliva and blood. The mixture ran down his chin. He coughed violently and sent glass shards across the curiously stained carpet.

Calvin pushed a hand across his head to straighten his hair. "You think it hurts now, wait until it comes out the other end."

"Let's go," Tucker said.

Calvin leaned forward and lifted a stack of cash off the pile. "And I'll have this for my trouble. You're welcome for the rest."

He put the money in his pocket as he stepped over Randy's heaving, hacking body. Tucker urged him along by grabbing hold of his elbow and pushing him like a manager removing an unruly older man from a Denny's during the early bird special.

As he passed by, Calvin kicked Brent's leg starting the wailing all over again.

They drove in silence until they crossed the river again. Something about being out of Illinois lifted the cone of silence.

"Well, they didn't know shit, did they?" Calvin said.

"No."

"Bit of a wasted trip."

"I guess so."

Calvin twisted his neck, trying to crack it. He'd be sore in the morning.

"Sorry about that," he said.

"Yeah," Tucker said. Inside he felt a small sense of relief. Calvin had been holding the news of Webb's disappearance so quietly inside Tucker couldn't be sure if he took it seriously. He'd seen the crack in the veneer. The man's son was missing. If anything, Calvin knew how serious the situation was much more so than Tucker.

They drove with the windows open, an attempt to get the drug den smell out of their noses. Tucker looked down at the water, watching the slow moving flow amble south to the Missouri.

12

Tucker tried his best to work the lock quickly to make it inside for the ringing phone. He left the keys in the lock as he pushed in to grab the phone off the kitchen counter.

"Hello?"

Idiot hadn't bothered to check the caller ID.

"Tucker, what the hell is going on over there?" Jenny. Pissed off.

"Not now, Jenny."

"Yes, now. You kidnapped my son."

Tucker slapped on the light, the fluorescent bulbs struggled to life. "Come on, Jen. Don't say shit like that. He came here on his own. Unannounced, I might add."

"Well, he's back home now. Ron picked him up at school before you could get your hands on him again."

"I thought only family was allowed to pick the kids up."

"I added Ron to the list. He's practically family." Practically because if Jenny and Ron got married it would end Tucker's alimony payments.

Calvin dropped the keys onto the counter and eavesdropped on Tucker's end of the call. He opened the refrigerator and

81

searched the shelves fruitlessly for a hidden beer.

"Jenny, if Milo wants to stay here every now and then I don't think it's a bad thing. Maybe you should look at why he wanted to come over here. It's not like I have an Xbox and a hot tub. There must be something he really doesn't like at your house."

Calvin shut the refrigerator door. Spoke loud enough for her to hear: "Like your whiny voice or your face." Tucker waved an angry hand for him to shut up.

"My condo, Tucker. I can't even afford a house to give this boy."

"I'll tell him to let you know next time he comes over. You can't keep him away from his own father though. He'll hate you for it."

"Among other things!" Calvin spoke up from behind the pantry door, still foraging for beer, even warm.

Tucker shook his head, squeezed his eyes tight. "Look, it's been a long day. He's safe at your place now. Let him cool off and maybe we can all sit down together and work out a new visitation plan. Huh?"

Jenny hung up. Tucker took the phone down from his ear, wondering how many more polite conversations he had in him before he erupted and made her eat one of her martini glasses. Another McGraw skill passed down through the generations.

"We need beer," Calvin said.

"I can go to the gas station and—"

"We need to make a stop too. But beer first."

Calvin picked the keys up off the counter and headed out of the kitchen.

"Wait, where are we going?"

"To see Hugh Stanley. But first, beer."

***

After waiting ten minutes outside of Hugh's office Calvin was steamed. When he and Tucker were finally waved in by the blonde at the door Calvin shifted into high gear. All Tucker could do was hold on.

Hugh sat behind his desk with a stack of papers before him like a regular businessman. Calvin came at him like a bar fight about to start.

"Those two dipshits didn't know squat. You're gonna need to start telling me a little more than you are, Hugh."

Hugh responded in kind. "Calm down there, Cal. I don't know no more than you."

"Well, then you don't know shit."

"No, I don't. Webb up and vanished into thin air."

"A man don't just disappear."

"Well, this one did." Hugh threw down the gold pen in his hand. "Cal, I respect that Webb is your son and all but you gotta understand what he took from me was mighty valuable. I want him found."

Calvin stood over the desk. Tucker lingered a few feet back, his usual position. He was getting so good at standing back and observing the goings on he ought to have taken up sketching.

Hugh said, "I'm sorry none of us are detective enough to track him down but last I checked we both lived our lives on the other side of the fence from those deductifying types."

"Put Kirby on it."

The mention of the name sucked the air out of the room. Out of Hugh at least. Calvin stood tall and waited for a response, he knew he'd thrown a grenade, but he wasn't sure if he'd pulled the pin.

Tucker shifted on his feet and the floorboards groaned. He didn't dare move.

"Kirby ain't currently taking on assignments."

Kirby Stanley, the black sheep. When all else failed you called Kirby. Fifteen years Hugh's junior he was raised on a steady diet of beatings and insults from his three older brothers. Grew him up mean. The business angles in the Stanley corporation had all been claimed by the elders leaving only the task of lead muscle. With a lot to prove, Kirby set out to be old reliable.

The legend grew. Rumor was he'd do anything. Some said he ate the heart of a man he killed once. Ate it in front of his family.

One story went that all he did was look at a man on his shit list and the boy up and died of a heart attack. Kirby Stanley could kill a man with his stare.

Most of it, if not all, was pure bullshit but legends never grew from the truth.

"Why not?" Calvin asked.

"Kirby and I... we had a falling out of sorts." Calvin's posture and sneer told Hugh he needed more than that. "He went up for a few. Some stupid domestic thing. He beat on a girl he was with. Got ten and served seven. When he came out he was a changed man. I mean, Kirby never was one for social graces or conversation. But since then... I don't know. He wasn't a help to business matters anymore."

"So we got dick is what you're saying?"

"I suppose so. Now what's this I hear about you making one of them boys eat glass?"

"He wasn't cooperating."

"And you took some of his money?"

"Ten grand off the top. He was aggravating me."

Hugh reclined in his leather CEO chair. "Cal, I gotta tell you, I'm disappointed. Used to be the McGraw name meant reliable. Now I got Webb running off with my truck, I got you coming in here and shouting and spittin' at me. I got you feeding people glass. I got this one," he pointed to Tucker. "What was your name again?"

"Tucker."

"Why are you even here?"

Calvin finally moved his feet, began pacing the area in front of Hugh's desk. "He's Webb's son. Ain't that enough?"

"No, frankly. It's not. I don't know if you remember, but I hired you boys on. I need to know if I can count on you."

"We've done your jobs so far, haven't we?"

"I suppose."

"Somehow I got a feeling I'm gonna be working off the debt of what's in that truck to my dying day."

Hugh sighed. Calvin watched him struggle to keep business over friendship, or at least fake a struggle.

"I've got some guys in other states looking for the truck. He's not in Iowa anymore. Not unless he's an idiot."

"He's no idiot," Calvin said. Hugh nodded slowly.

"I got another job for you. If you want it."

Calvin looked at Tucker. Tucker shrugged. Calvin knew the boy was being pushed beyond his normal limits but he also knew the McGraw inside wasn't near the ragged edge yet. The boy needed to push himself a little further.

"What's the gig?"

"You're gonna need a different car. I don't know what the hell kind of clown car you've got now but it won't do for this

85

one."

"You got one?"

Hugh laughed. "I got six but you can't have any. You figure it out."

13

"I don't want to know, do I?" Tucker stared at the black Lincoln Town Car in the driveway the way a parent looked at a report card full of Ds and Fs.

Calvin shut the door, turned to admire his new acquisition. "I suspect you don't. No."

"If the Stanley's can't tell us anything about Dad, why are we still working for them?"

"You know a better way to work off that ten million? You want to offer to shine his shoes for him? Pick up his coffee in the morning? Tell you what, he's got a blond for that and she sucks his dick too. You willing to step up?"

Tucker kicked a pebble on the ground.

"I didn't think so." Calvin hitched up his pants. "You about ready?"

"I guess." Tucker climbed in the passenger seat, a boy on the way to the dentist. Pouting and letting the world know he disapproved of how his evening was being spent. Being in the front seat with him, Calvin felt the heat of his stewing.

"Tucker," Calvin said, perching his arm in the open window. "I know you don't think much of the family business. And I know you don't much care for being dragged into it this way. But let me tell you, wherever your dad is, when he hears how you stuck with it to try to find him, well, he's gonna be mighty impressed."

"What if he's dead?"

The words came out on a thick cloud of noxious fumes. The stink of something long fermented, left to rot for too many days. Someone should have said it sooner.

Calvin turned and spit out the window, a foul taste in his mouth all of a sudden.

The Lincoln hummed along on soft shocks. The velour seats cradled the men in armchair comfort even at 50 miles an hour. Over the fields to his right the sun fell to eye level with Tucker. The bruised orange hung over the flatlands, dipping behind a silo and diffusing the dying light behind trees whose branches appeared black against the glow. Tucker could stare at the sun. It wasn't high noon overhead sun that would burn your eyesight away, it was the kind of sunset that oceans made prettier but Midwesterners made do with. The Iowa version of pretty.

"I tell you what," Calvin said. "He made off with that truck, let's say. He'd lay low. He's not gonna go calling you, me or anyone else until he reaches his destination. And even then he might wait a while. He knows these Stanleys better n' anyone. A McGraw man never leaves no trail of breadcrumbs leading anywhere."

Tucker was beginning to get real tired of hearing what a McGraw man did and didn't do.

"This is the job, huh? Driving out to some random, isolated place in the dark. Picking up drugs. Taking them somewhere else. Mailmen with more expensive packages. Is that it?"

"You think what you like. Never seen a mailman in short pants have to outrun the law. Or worse—an outlaw."

"Never seen a mailman kill anybody either."

"Well, then Tuck, you're not paying attention."

Deep in the bowels of Johnson County the Lincoln bounced over a rutted road out to a house that once would have been owned by a farmer and his family. Honest working men and women up at five A.M., growing their own food and food for others. Now, the two story house earned another living as a thriving methamphetamine lab.

Ten years of reaping, sowing, milking, tilling, sweating would earn as much money as the lab could make in a month.

Calvin parked by an oak tree. The two men got out and both noticed the sweet manure smell of the Iowa countryside had been replaced by a stinging chemical tang. Chances of stepping in anything and ruining your shoes had been reduced, but even if every hog in the yard was sick with swine flu you'd never have to wear a gas mask like the men working inside.

They hadn't been trying for stealth so the headlights moving up the long drive gave them away minutes ago. By the time both Tucker and Calvin were out of the car the activity had started inside.

Hoarse, overused voices shouted commands. The door burst open and a line of men marched single file onto the covered porch. Tucker watched them move like an infantry. He doubted they'd come outside to set a spell and drink lemonade.

Seven men altogether, Hispanic, hands on top of their heads with fingers interlaced. Some had breathing masks dangling around their necks. Behind them came the shouters.

Three men with shotguns, dressed in black. A fourth man came from the house but Tucker could still hear movement inside, and destruction.

The fourth man carried a pistol and he passed quickly by the prisoners and stepped off the porch, bound for Calvin and Tucker.

Calvin kept eyes on the man, spoke to Tucker. "This'll be Rudy."

Rudy didn't bother with introductions. "Pop the trunk. My guys will load you up."

"Fill the back seat first," Calvin said. "I like my load where I can see it."

"So can the cops."

Calvin turned his body flat to Rudy. "Look at me, son. At my age do you think I've made it this far by lettin' cops see what I'm carrying?"

Rudy was either in a hurry or sufficiently impressed to give in.

"Let's move!" he shouted and moved back toward the porch.

A new line of men, also dressed in black, stepped out of the house each carrying an armload of tightly wrapped bundles. Silver duct tape sealed them all the size of two footballs sewn together. Each of the three men carried three bundles.

Calvin opened the back door of the Lincoln for them.

Tucker kept his eyes on the seven men, now on their knees, lined up on the porch. The shotguns hovered close to their temples, moving man to man down the line making sure everyone felt the aim of twin barrels. The seven men stayed still and obeyed.

The porch light silhouetted their figures so Tucker could not read fear in anyone's eyes. He saw by the swaying movement of their bodies that their knees were starting to hurt on the rough wood of the porch.

When the first deposit of drugs had been made in the car, the trio turned back to the house for another load. Alone again for a moment Tucker whispered to Calvin.

"What's going on?"

"Looks like a takeover." Calvin eyed the prisoners as well. "Stanley's men are shutting down this lab, taking the finished product and closing up shop."

"Closing up shop? What does that mean?"

"You really have to ask?"

The same three men walked the same path down to the car with a new armload of bundles, depositing them in the backseat of the Lincoln.

Three more loads went in until any more would start to block Calvin's view out the back.

"How much more?" he asked one of the movers after the fifth delivery.

"A bunch."

Calvin pressed a button under the dash and the trunk yawned open.

Upstairs, Tucker saw orange. The glow reminded him of the sun that had wisely moved on to another part of the world. He recognized the slow dancing movements of color as fire.

Three windows from three different bedrooms ran across the top floor. Gables arched over the end two. Each window lit up a few seconds after the previous until three glowing rectangles shone in the darkened sky.

Tucker put a hand on Calvin's arm. "Delivery is one thing, but this?"

"Another test."

"What else do they need to know about us?"

"I don't know. Maybe it's that the job has changed since I was in it. Running cases of moonshine liquor was a bunch of laughs back then. All we had after us was the keystone cops. I could count the number of guys I saw killed on one hand. Now..."

Calvin kept his eyes on the porch. Counted to seven. Touched the tips of his fingers one by one.

The next load went into the trunk and the men immediately spun and went back for another. Rudy stepped down off the porch and returned to the car.

"Almost there."

Calvin lifted his chin towards the porch. "Then what?"

"Then you deliver this stuff."

Tucker's eyes were watching the fire grow and reach into the attic. "Then you all gonna sit down and roast marshmallows?"

Rudy looked past Calvin to Tucker, almost seeing him for the first time. He didn't answer. They exchanged disapproving stares.

Calvin spoke up as casually as if they were standing on the banks of a pond fishing and drinking beers. "You know anything about Webb McGraw?"

"McGraw? The driver?"

"Yeah. Went missing."

"Not what I heard."

Tucker's eyes leapt away from the fire to Rudy. The glow of the flames reached down across the yard and gave him the orange features of a man telling ghost stories around a campfire.

"What did you hear?" Calvin asked, calm as you please.

"That truck was stolen. And Webb, well shit, he's—"

A pop and crackle of glass interrupted the story as the middle window in the upstairs burst from the heat.

All eyes went up to the roof line. Mistake.

Tucker wasn't sure who, but one of the seven took the distraction and used it. A shotgun was quickly liberated and put to use. The blast of even a single barrel put to shame the weak tinkling of glass from the window.

A black-clad body fell from the porch. The remaining six Hispanic men managed to move in a dozen directions at once. The two other shotguns were similarly confiscated and two more eruptions filled the night air.

Tucker crouched and spun in place, unsure where to go.

Calvin ducked behind the back end of the Lincoln, grateful for stealing an American car with a thick hide and no concern over gas mileage or weight to power ratios. The panels on a Lincoln were one step away from armored.

Calvin was joined by Rudy, his pistol drawn and ready. They watched as the seven prisoners charged back inside the house where the three moving men, and the upstairs arsonists, would be.

The farmhouse became a shooting gallery.

Calvin turned to Rudy. "What did you hear about Webb?"

"What? Let's get the fuck out of here!"

"Tell me what you heard about Webb McGraw."

"Are you fuckin' nuts? They'll kill us. Get in and drive." Rudy stayed low and started to move toward the open back door. Calvin grabbed the back of his shirt and pulled him off his crouched feet. He spun Rudy around and pushed his back into the tire of the Lincoln, their bodies hidden by the open door. Gunfire inside the house gave away who was winning the fight. Shotguns: 1. Arms full of drug bundles: 0.

"You tell me what you know or I kill you here and now."

"Granddad!" Tucker scrambled along the passenger side of the car feeling alone and unprotected.

Rudy looked into Calvin's serious eyes. "I'll tell you on the way. Let's go!"

A load of buckshot peppered the Lincoln. Calvin grabbed the front of Rudy's shirt.

"Tucker, get in!"

Tucker froze his progress around the back and retreated to the passenger door, grateful for the instruction.

Calvin pulled Rudy along, away from the back seat, filled with tight bundles. He grunted as he lifted Rudy up and pushed him forward into the open trunk.

Rudy, shocked, fell into the deep well of carpeted storage. Roomy enough for two sets of golf clubs, the sales pitch went.

Calvin slapped a hand over Rudy's gun and pulled it free. He turned the barrel on the frightened man. "Next time, you answer me on the first go 'round."

Another shotgun blast tore into the hood of the car. In the front seat Tucker squeezed himself onto the floor.

Calvin slammed the trunk shut. Rudy's "NO—" was cut off.

Calvin raised the gun and fired off five quick shots in the general vicinity of the front porch. The noise was enough to make two shotgun-toting ex-prisoners dive for cover even if none of the shots landed anywhere that would do harm.

Calvin slid behind the wheel of the Lincoln and powered the engine to life. He dropped the gear lever into R and had a brief moment of panic when he turned and saw only an empty passenger seat. He looked down and noticed Tucker curled up on the floor mat and stomped down on the gas.

He reversed the Lincoln down the dirt drive, turning his head over the back seat and away from the house where the two men were up and shooting again. He quickly receded into the night and the buckshot did no harm at that distance.

There were damn good reasons the Daytona 500 wasn't run in reverse. As a gear—it sucked.

The Lincoln weaved from edge to edge of the dirt driveway on a drunken retreat barely hitting fifteen miles an hour. Calvin had to turn her around to do any serious getting away.

He cut the wheel and the car made a wide arc, bouncing over the rough embankments of the path. The trunk of the car backed into a mess of overgrown bushes and the metal echoed with the pounding of a hundred sticks and branches. Rudy cried out from the trunk, the sound a confusing din of unknown threats.

Calvin brought the lever down to D and laid his foot hard on the gas. The tires spun and the car lurched forward, but then fell back into the comfort of the tangle of bushes.

Tucker looked up from the floor. "Are we stuck?"

Calvin ignored him. He dropped the lever into second gear and pressed more gently on the gas this time. The car moved forward, the front raised as the tires reached the top of the small mound separating yard from driveway, then gravity pulled them back like the bushes held a firm grip with ten thousand spindly fingers.

Tucker got himself off the floor and into the front seat. He looked back toward the house and saw two pairs of headlights swinging into line as both vehicles found the top of the drive.

Calvin had the steady focus of a surgeon, his mind melding with the engine, imploring the machine to do what he asked.

Once more the Lincoln rocked forward on the soft shock absorbers and teased them before being pulled back into the bush. The pitch on Rudy's voice rose and octave with each failed attempt.

"They're coming," Tucker said.

"I know it," Calvin said.

Four dots of white stuttered along the uneven dirt path as they approached. One more attempt and the best they could hope for would be a T-bone collision with one of the cars.

The lever came down again, engaged R. The car powered through the bush. Branches clawed at the car from beneath and ran brittle talons over the sides, strong enough to carve lines in the paint and tear loose the side view mirror on Tucker's side.

The noise was like marbles in a blender, but the Lincoln bumped over the last bush and again hit flat ground. Soft grass cushioned the ride but made for poor grip on the tires. It didn't matter much because neither of the two cars followed. Tucker watched as the two sets of headlights ran parallel to the Lincoln as Calvin tried to keep the weaving to a minimum.

Visibility was awful. They ran over an old tree stump and Calvin thought sure they'd cracked the rear axel but the car kept running.

Calvin cut the wheel sharply when he spotted the T-shaped meeting of driveway and country lane. The wheels spun and kicked up grass. Calvin smiled a bit; his version of mowing the lawn.

He dropped the car into drive and banged up onto the paved road.

The two vehicles following them, one a four-door sedan and the other a pickup truck, made a wide turn onto the road as well.

"About time we had ourselves a decent run at this," Calvin said. "Let's see what they've got."

What they had were shotguns. A powerful boom sounded behind them followed by the thinner sound of buckshot hitting the thick American steel on the back end of the Lincoln.

Calvin already had the V-8 pushing forty-five and winding up for more.

"The glove box," he said to Tucker.

"What?"

"In the glove box. Get the gun."

Tucker was tempted to look around and see who else Calvin could have possibly been speaking to. He opened the glove compartment and saw Calvin's weathered gun. He left it inside.

Calvin urged the car over sixty.

"Well? Use it."

"For what?"

"Shoot back!"

Another blast of a shotgun filled the night, still not as loud as the branches scraping the car.

Calvin began to cut wide arcs across both lanes of the country highway. The swerving kept his speed down, but made for a moving target.

He turned to Tucker. "Shoot at their tires or just shoot in their direction. They'll get the point. I might be able to break away if you can slow them down."

Tucker turned back to the open glove box, saw out the windshield instead.

"Watch it!"

Calvin was aimed at a fence post blocking an access road on the left of the highway. He swung the Lincoln around with a squeal of the tires.

"Pay attention," Tucker said. Calvin did not appreciate the driving advice.

"Just use the damn gun."

Using Calvin's lapse of attention, the sedan pulled up to their rear door, edging closer with the front bumper.

Tucker lifted the gun out of the compartment. He turned over his shoulder to see the rear window of the sedan open and the long barrel of a shotgun poke out and aim down at their tires.

Calvin pressed a button on his door and Tucker's window powered down. The sudden blast of air snapped Tucker into action. He thrust the gun out the window and fired a shot into the hood of the sedan.

It punched a hole in the sheet metal and the driver swerved to the right. The shotgun barrel retreated inside the car.

Tucker pulled his gun inside too and looked down at it. He hadn't fired a gun since he was ten, and that was at cans. He wasn't aiming for anything in particular so he was glad to have hit anything at all.

"I think I know this area," Calvin said. "Used to be an old moonshine shack up here not too far."

"I think we need to get to town."

"No, we can lose him in the backwoods. That's McGraw country."

The sedan came roaring back, the driver accelerating and backing off, thrusting forward then retreating with whining complaints from the tiny engine.

Tucker raised the gun again, tried to find the sight and

focus on a target but the car was moving too much.

"Here it is."

Tucker banged into the door as Calvin cut the wheel hard to the left. Tires squealed in a discordant harmony as all three cars changed course.

Calvin speared the Lincoln off onto a short access road. His eyes squinted as he drove, trying to dredge up memories of secret paths and shortcuts. Instead he saw a semi-trailer, rusted out and tires flat, painted with JESUS SAVES on the side, completely blocking the roadway.

"Aw, shit. This ain't it."

The wheels of the Lincoln bit the dirt as he turned a sloppy U, kicking up dust that came in through the window to choke Tucker.

The sedan and the pickup each split off in opposite directions as the trio dug trenches into ground that hadn't seen a car in decades.

"Do you know where you're going?" Tucker asked.

"Shut up."

The chasing sedan proved more nimble in getting back to the highway and by the time they had gotten back up to speed he was neck and neck with the Lincoln. Tucker could see the crazed eyes of the driver, a man who had stared death in the face not ten minutes earlier. His rage was focused completely on the Lincoln.

Tucker did his best to aim at the front tire of the sedan. He fired a round and it punctured the front panel of the sedan, but the tires kept spinning. The driver had seen through Tucker, saw his inexperience. He didn't veer away, he kept his car straight and true and the nose of the shotgun began sniffing the air again.

Tucker closed one eye and squinted his other as he tried to sight down the barrel. Calvin swung right and brought the two cars together like sumo wrestlers when the whistle blows.

Tucker barely got his arm inside the window in time to keep it from being crushed.

"Jesus Christ. Tell me if you're gonna do that."

Both cars resumed their course. Spring cornfields rushed by on either side with low stalks thirsty for rain. The lights from distant farmhouses nothing more than stars on the horizon. The road curved slowly to the left, a rarity in a state laid out in grids.

Tucker fired again. The front tire on the sedan exploded in a burst of flaccid rubber. The sedan pulled quickly at an angle and the back end swung out. The driver kept the car from flipping, but it slid down off the highway into a drainage ditch running alongside the cornfield. The sedan landed hard and the sound of metal folding in on itself carried out over the field.

One down.

The lights of a town glowed ahead. The curve of the road straightened and the beacon ahead called, offering 24 hour gas and drive-through hamburgers.

The headlights of the pickup truck stared hi-beams through the back window on the Lincoln.

"We get up here and I can outmaneuver him in the streets," Calvin said.

Tucker looked at his granddad. Hunched over the wheel, eyes straining, brow furrowed. He did not instill the confidence that having a McGraw behind the wheel should.

It was obvious to Tucker, as much as Calvin wanted to still be the best, his days were behind him. He wondered if Calvin felt the same thing.

The pickup breathed heavy on their back like a lion on the hunt. Tucker thought how glad he was they weren't in an Impala. The coincidence would have been too much.

Calvin strained to see street signs as the edge of town came up on them fast. These Midwest horse towns all smeared out on the edges like soft clay. A few streets, then the first street light, lucky if you got two or three. A gas station, a market, a liquor store —always a liquor store—and then before you knew it the smear began again and you were back in the corn fields. And that's even when you were not doing seventy.

The town was already asleep. Stop signs meant nothing.

"Here's where I lose him."

Calvin cut the wheel again, the grin of confidence back on his lips. The pickup followed but lost ground on a sloppy turn. The heavier, bulkier truck was no match for the Lincoln, even though Calvin was wishing for the Bandit right then.

If that old girl was under him they would have burned these clowns ten miles back.

Off the main drag the streets were dark. The squint returned to Calvin's face and Tucker started scanning the view for anything to help his granddad.

They began to run out of road quickly. This was no giant maze to get lost in, this was a one horse town.

Calvin turned up one street, headed back down towards the main road. The pickup swerved and had trouble sticking to the corners like Calvin, but he stayed persistently, annoyingly in the rearview.

Calvin powered forward putting more distance between them. They reached the main road through town and Calvin swung left, continuing back on his route and pointed out of town.

"Okay, maybe I can lose him on the straightaway. I've got more engine than him I think."

Tucker had never heard his granddad say maybe before when it came to driving.

Up ahead a horn blasted. Tucker jumped and looked for oncoming traffic, but saw none. The sound signaled again.

A train.

"I can make it."

"No, you can't. Turn around."

"I can make it."

"Granddad!"

A half mile ahead lay train tracks. The endless nighttime moan of cross country trains rambling across the flat Midwestern plains used to comfort Tucker as he lay in bed. A mile away from where he grew up was a route which ran through after dark carrying a hundred cars of corn and soybeans and hogs. The deep chorus of air horn blasts reminded Tucker every night that there were tracks leading out of Iowa. The train song became his lullabye.

It was about to become his death march.

"You have any idea how many trains I outran in my day?"

Tucker felt certain whatever the number was, he wasn't going to add to it tonight.

The lights on the train stretched back as far as they could see. A hundred cars. More? Two engines up front did the pulling and even though the train ambled across the fields at a comfortable cruise not above forty-five, stopping that much tonnage would take five miles at least.

The speedometer on the Lincoln climbed north of fifty. The pickup matched them.

"Goddammit, Granddad, you can't make that."

"Yes, I can."

By the time Tucker could see the gates, they were down. The red lights flashed and a bell rang, but out of habit more than anything.

The Lincoln's headlights swept over the crossing and Calvin did the math.

"Nope. Not gonna happen."

Both feet went on the brake. Much as Calvin loved his Bandit, he was grateful for anti-lock brakes. The tires skidded and chirped along the asphalt as the car gripped and slid, gripped then slid some more.

When the car stopped Calvin immediately dropped gears into R and spun his torso around to look out the back window.

"What the hell are you doing?" Tucker demanded. "You'll kill us."

"He'll move."

The pickup accelerated down the main drag. What the air horn or the spinning red lights on the crossing couldn't do, the sight of a Lincoln Town Car reversing toward them at full speed did. The pickup hit the brakes.

Committed to a brake-locking slide, the truck was unable to veer out of the path of the backwards Lincoln.

"He'll swerve," Calvin said. A split second later his good sense caught up with him and said he would not. Calvin also hit the brakes.

The two vehicles ground hot rubber into the asphalt of the sleepy town and slowed from their highly illegal top speeds, but still collided at a forceful clip. As the two vehicles hit, Tucker heard a pop and thought the back tires must have blown.

The Lincoln was shoved forward about ten feet but then crunched to a stop again, the pickup now nosed into its back end.

The train rolled by ahead of them, steady and rhythmic. Headed for other states, other adventures.

The pickup rolled backward, the driver's foot having come off the brake.

Both vehicles sat, unmoving, as Tucker, disoriented from the crash and still in shock, counted out twenty-three train cars go by.

"You okay?" Calvin asked.

Tucker hadn't thought about it yet. He did a quick personal inventory. "Yeah. You?" Calvin didn't answer.

"Gimme that." Calvin took the gun out of Tucker's hand and stepped out of the car. Tucker got out as well.

Calvin approached slowly, the steady metal on metal sounds of the train masking his footsteps crunching on the pavement. "You were supposed to swerve, asshole." There was no movement inside the truck.

As he passed, Calvin turned to the crumpled wreckage of the Lincoln's trunk. He turned his eyes back to the pickup.

Tucker had reached the passenger side. The man inside slowly rotated his head as if he couldn't believe it was still attached. Blood seeped from his nose and his ears and a growing knot on his forehead. Across his lap lay a shotgun, the barrel pointed at the driver whose face was a cherry red mass of open skin and exposed muscle. The pop he heard. The gun going off during the impact.

Calvin came around to Tucker's side, saw the man still moving. He pushed Tucker back and extended the gun. Tucker raised a hand to protest but no words came out to go with it.

Calvin squeezed the trigger. An empty click. The gun hovered for a moment. The man in the passenger seat didn't notice anyone else was there.

Calvin gripped the gun in his fist and punched out, clipping the passenger across the nose with the butt of the gun and knocking him out. Calvin grunted from the effort and lost his balance. He managed to right himself but looked every bit his age in doing so. The noises he made, the grunting and groaning, seemed involuntary.

He straightened, put a hand to his lower back then turned and walked to the Lincoln.

They both stood by the rear of the car. Neither one asked if they thought Rudy would be okay inside. The origami metal of the trunk said no, as did the flow of blood dripping from the corner like drool from a St. Bernard.

Calvin put the gun back in Tucker's hand, inspected the back tires, assuring they had enough clearance from the damage to continue on. They did.

They both waited in silence as the train lumbered on for another seven minutes. Once it was gone and silence fell across the plains again, Calvin turned to Tucker.

"Let's go make this delivery."

He didn't need to tell Tucker that was the job. Make the delivery at all costs. Do your best to explain the body in the trunk, the carnage at the farmhouse.

But deliver the goods.

14

Calvin was right. There were questions to be sure: about the body in the trunk. About the shootout at the farmhouse. But most important on the Stanley family agenda was the delivery of those bundles of drugs.

Tucker did not stay nearby when they muscled the trunk open with crowbars. Took three men to wedge it open. They would have left it, left Rudy inside, if not for the load of crystal meth crushed beneath the body.

Only one bag had split and Calvin thought he heard one of the men say something about salvaging the load.

They left the Lincoln with the delivery and got a ride home, stopping off for beer on the way.

By the time they arrived back at Tucker's place it was 1:30 in the morning and Milo was asleep on the couch, a note pinned to him reading: DON'T BE PISSED. IT'S YOUR WEEKEND.

Tucker cursed to himself. He couldn't remember that last time he'd looked at a calendar. He'd completely forgotten it was his court-appointed weekend with his son.

Hugh Stanley's breakfast was interrupted.

"They did what?"

"All seven of them. Went fucking nuts and shot up the place. Our guys already had the fire going so it's toast now but at least three of them got away we think."

"Cal took out the rest?"

"Looks like it. Picked up a police report this morning about two cars with Mexicans in them holding shotguns. All dead."

"Any link to us?"

"Not so far. As soon as the old man and his partner told us about it we sent some guys out to clear out our guys' bodies from the house. We got three but the others were inside and burned so bad they couldn't even tell what was a person or not."

Hugh set down his orange juice. "And the guy in the trunk?"

"One of ours. The old man said the pickup hit him from behind."

"Yeah, but what was he doing in the trunk?"

"Said they were trying to escape. It must have been crazy out there. The car had shotgun pellets all over it."

Hugh thought for a moment. "But the load made it?"

"Yeah. Good size too. We're cutting it right now."

"Good, good." Hugh picked up his juice again, drained the last of it. "We fucking need that."

***

Calvin entered from the kitchen, pulling his first beer at 8:30 in the morning. "You ready to go?"

"Go where?" Tucker asked.

"To see Hugh. That Rudy was about to tell me something about Webb. I don't think Hugh has been up front with us."

"No way. You can go without me. I've had enough."

"Suit yourself." Calvin tipped the beer and gulped the last two-thirds.

Tucker looked closer at Calvin. Unshowered, hair a mess of gray angles and cowlicks, eyes unfocused. He wasn't drunk but, same as he had the night before, he looked every inch of his age. And after the less-than-stellar display of the fabled McGraw driving skills Tucker had lost confidence in his granddad as a trustworthy representative of their case.

It made Tucker a little sad. Like meeting a celebrity without makeup. They weren't the golden heroes you once thought.

"Okay, I'll go. But I drive." Tucker eyeballed the empty beer in Calvin's hand. Calvin looked down and saw the can as if for the first time. He tipped it again to see if there was any beer hiding in the bottom of the can before setting it on the side table.

Tucker looked at his son, felt a hundred different ways he was failing him in his attempts to shield him from the family business. "You wait here."

***

Calvin entered Hugh's office unannounced again.

"This is getting old, Cal."

"You're telling me."

Tucker was closer behind this time. Hugh noticed the younger man as more than a tagalong, an unsevered Siamese twin that came with Calvin no matter where he went.

The two men crowded the front of Hugh's desk. "Sit, boys. We can talk better once you take a load off."

Calvin sat in one of the two armchairs facing Hugh's desk. Tucker stayed standing.

"I'm obliged to you for that situation last night," Hugh said.

"Oh, you mean the unholy shitstorm you sent us in to?" Calvin may have sat down, but his attitude still loomed over Hugh's desk like a vulture on a branch.

"How the hell am I supposed to know the Mexicans are gonna go apeshit out there? They were all supposed to be dead by the time you got there."

"They weren't."

With each meeting it took less time for Hugh to become exasperated. "What do you want, Cal?"

"One of your guys said he knew something about Webb. Made it seem like he didn't run away."

"What did he say?"

"I don't recall exactly. Just that there was more to the story."

"So ask him."

"You know damn well they're all dead."

"Well, then what the fuck am I supposed to do about it?"

Tucker put out his hands in a calming gesture. "Okay, everyone settle down."

Hugh pushed back from his desk, his leather chair banging the wall behind him. He ran a hand through his hair. "Goddammit, Cal, you don't know the other shit I've got on my mind right now. Things aren't like when we were coming up."

"Don't give me the old things ain't what they used to be speech."

"They're not. There's competition. The overhead is greater. The talent pool is shrinking. Any backwoods jerk-off with internet access can cook his own drugs these days. I'm like those musicians who used to make millions and now everyone is swapping songs for free online. I'm down and out, Cal. Why do you think I'm shutting down the competition?" His anger grew and the stress showed on his skin like a rash.

"They're like cockroaches. Stamp one out and three more crawl up from south of the border. That score last night is gonna help keep me in business for a month. After that, who knows? That's why I needed that truck that Webb ran off with. Needed it bad, Cal."

"Hugh, I'm real sorry and all, but how is this my fault?"

Hugh pounded on the desk. "Because your fucking son took my last best shot is why."

"We still don't know that," Tucker said. Hugh turned his anger on him.

"Unless you can prove to me otherwise, it's a fact. You can fuck you're innocent until proven guilty. That might work in your world but when you live your life surrounded by criminals, if you think they might have possibly, maybe there's a small chance they fucked you—they did."

Tucker took the abuse. He didn't shrink like normal. Years of Jenny stiffening his backbone? Or days of Calvin?

"So that's why," Hugh said, "you'll keep working off your debt to me. Because I believe in responsibility. I believe in family. And I believe in getting what I'm promised, no matter who promised it."

The door behind them opened. Two of Stanley's larger assistants filled the doorway. Calvin turned to them, took the hint, then turned back to Hugh and stood.

"No more shitstorms, okay? And you hear from any of your guys about Webb, you let me know first."

"You keep doing what you're doing. I'm serious, Cal. You did me right last night. I don't forget that." Hugh lowered his chin, stared at Calvin through low eyebrows and heavy eyelids. "I don't forget anything."

Calvin and Tucker let themselves be escorted to the door.

Hugh, for his parting words, said, "And stop coming by my office without an appointment."

15

Tucker drove. Calvin fumed as he stared out his window.

"Sounds like they're really hurting for money, huh?" Tucker said.

"Bullshit," Calvin said. "They cry poverty all the damn time. If they went around talking about how much money they had coming out of their asses then everyone who worked for them would want a bigger share."

"I guess so."

"Wanna go to a shooting range?" Calvin asked. "Let's go to a shooting range."

"No." In high school Tucker's nickname was 'Buzzkill'. True story.

Calvin spat out his window for no other reason than it felt good. "Well, the way I'm feeling it's either that or a prostitute."

"No one is going shooting or to see a prostitute for Christ's sake."

"Come to think of it, Tuck, it might do you some good."

Tucker scowled at his granddad. "I won't even ask which one you are referring to." Tucker thought that was the end of it. He was wrong.

"The whore." Calvin continued to look out his window, pouting.

The rest of the afternoon Calvin sulked around the house like a teenager. He drained four beers while watching ESPN and ignoring his grandson and great-grandson.

Around seven o'clock Calvin ran out of beer.

"I'm going out."

"You're not driving," Tucker said.

"Why the hell not?"

"Because you've had too much to drink. In fact, I think you're all done with the beer for tonight."

"Who the fuck are you, my priest?"

"No. But I think maybe you've had enough."

"Oh, you'll know it when I've had enough." Tucker didn't doubt it. "Fuck it, I'll walk."

Calvin pulled on his jacket. The Gas N Save was about a half mile down the road. Doable, even for a man his age. He seemed steady on his feet. It had been a slow but steady intake, not a mad rush to get drunk. If anything, thought Tucker, the air would get a little easier to breathe with some space between them.

"Fine. Call me if you can't make it back, okay? I'll come pick you up." He looked at Milo. "Maybe I'll even send Milo." Milo smiled.

"Yeah, I'll call you if I need you," Calvin said over his shoulder as he pushed out the door and shut it behind him louder than he needed to.

Tucker sighed. Milo watched his dad with a question on his lips.

"You want a pop or something?" Tucker asked.

"Sure."

"I think I got a Coke and Dr. Pepper."

"Whatever is fine."

Milo followed Tucker into the kitchen and they both pulled the tabs on cans of Coke. They each let the first swigs bite down their throats before exhaling loudly. Tucker had been wrong. The air was still quite thick.

"So," Milo started. "Is Grandpa really missing?"

Tucker took another sip and wished he had a splash of rum to mix with it.

"He's not returning any calls at least. I think he ran into some trouble at work and he's trying to sort it all out."

"Dad, I've been patient. You gotta admit." Tucker nodded. "Will you tell me what's going on around here. You stole a car. You and him and sneaking around to meetings. What gives?"

The way he dreaded the day he had to tell Milo about the divorce, Tucker felt a block of ice in his stomach. He swallowed another mouthful of Coke and nearly choked on it. The boy was right. Time to come clean. Time to let him know he was a McGraw.

Tucker started at the beginning.

By the time he got around to their current day problems Milo was out of breath. His family? Working for mobsters?

"Not mobsters," Tucker said. "Just criminals. This isn't The Godfather or anything. No one's even Italian. There's someone like the Stanley family in every state. And someone like the McGraws."

"But we're the best, right?" Milo had an eager smile on his face.

"No such thing. Milo, what your grandfathers do is wrong. They've been doing wrong for decades. It was up to me to break the cycle and now it's up to you to continue on the straight and narrow and not fall into their trap."

"Jesus, Dad, you sound like J. Edgar Hoover."

"Do you even know who that is?"

"FBI guy. Look, if Grandpa is missing then we have to find him."

"We're trying. But we're gonna try within the law."

"Then why are you working for the Stanleys."

Tucker drained his Coke, giving him a minute to think. Goddamn logic coming along and ruining everything.

"Right now we're using any method available. The important thing is, now you know the mistakes your grandfathers have made in life and you can see the trouble it's gotten them into. I don't want you to think of them like folk heroes or something. They're criminals. I don't want you to be like them. It's dangerous. I'm about to cut it off anyhow. We can't keep doing work for Stanley. It's not right."

"What about the money you owe him?"

"I don't know right now. I'll work it out."

The front door opened and Calvin stepped in, a fresh 12-pack under his arm.

"All you gotta do is walk like that every now and then to see why the hell they invented the car in the first place. If God had wanted us to use our feet he would have put wheels on them and an engine in our ass."

Milo smiled. Tucker managed to hide his smile.

***

Hugh Stanley reached for his desk lamp, done for the night. He rubbed his eyes and ran a hand over his hair, feeling how thin it had gotten, seemingly in the last six months. Christ, all those jack-offs on Wall Street didn't lose this much sleep over the money they lost. And that was shitload more than the debt Stanley faced. It was all relative.

A timid knock on the door halted Hugh's hand an inch from the pull chain on the lamp.

"C'mon in."

Wyatt stepped in. A Stanley by marriage when his dad hitched on to one of the two Stanley sisters. Hopelessly ugly girls with great big tits and an overeagerness to prove to men that they were talented beyond their looks. Henrietta and Olive Stanley popped the cherries of more guys in Iowa than any brothel west of the Mississippi. Most guys visited once and moved on, immediately assuming they could do better. Most of them should have stuck around for the practice.

Wyatt's father did stick around with Olive and he'd been a happy man. His astigmatism led many to assume that he had never in his life had sex with his own wife with his glasses on and that accounted for much of their happiness.

Wyatt had been a helpful up-and-comer and in recent years had moved into Hugh's inner circle of confidants, often times only by virtue of being the nearest warm body.

"You heading out?" Wyatt asked.

"Time to turn in."

"You think anymore about the McGraw deal?"

"I agree they're sniffing around like a dog in heat but what am I supposed to do?"

"Let me handle it."

"Handle it." He scoffed. "Still with so much to prove, huh Wyatt?" Wyatt's eyes swept the floor. "I can't go knocking off everyone who might hurt us. There'd be no one left. Besides,

I still say they can help us out."

"But at what price?"

"Less than what I would pay to anyone else and right now, that's key."

Hugh snapped off the desk lamp and walked to the door. Wyatt lifted the old man's overcoat off a coatrack and helped him on with it.

"Whatever you say, uncle Hugh. Just promise you'll let me know when you want me to take care of it."

"Oh, you'll be first to know." Hugh patted the kid's back, condescending. All these young guys loved playing gangster. The family didn't get where it was by thinking of themselves as tough guys and crooks. The Stanleys were businessmen and should act accordingly.

Hugh pulled a hat onto his head, protecting the thinning gray from the night chill. These kids, he thought. All the class went out of this business with the speakeasies.

Goddamn shame.

Despite the hat and overcoat a coldness grabbed him. The spooked feeling hit him somewhere down in the bottom of his spine. He stopped by the open car door Wyatt held for him and looked over his shoulder. Somewhere, out in the night, bad news was coming.

16

The police knocked at 6:30 A.M. Tucker's morning erection hadn't even faded.

He shouted from behind the closed door. "Who is it?"

"Police officer, Mr. McGraw. May we have a moment of your time?"

They weren't beating down the door, that had to be a good sign. The smell of cops sent Calvin rushing off the couch to the kitchen out of sight. Milo appeared at the entry to the hallway, his sleeping bag wrapped around him.

Tucker opened the door wondering how good he could be at lying and knowing he was about to find out.

"Mr. McGraw?" said one of two officers on the doorstep, both in blue uniforms and the speaker sporting a cop mustache while the other apparently hadn't gotten the memo.

"Yes." Tucker hadn't yet moved his body to invite them in.

"Is your father Webb McGraw, sir?"

The question spun Tucker's thinking 180°. "Yes. Why?"

The officer, Shultz read his name tag, removed his hat. Tucker knew why before he spoke.

"I'm afraid your father was found dead, sir."

From the kitchen Tucker heard the sound of a beer can cracking open.

"When?"

"This morning."

"Dead for sure?"

Shultz turned briefly to his partner who would not meet his eyes. "Yes, sir. He's been murdered. Homicide is on the case now."

Tucker wasn't sure if he should fake surprise. It certainly wasn't what he felt.

"Do they know who did it?"

"No, sir. The thing is..." again the partner would not throw Shultz a life line. "Only part of his body was found."

Tucker blinked twice. He didn't want to ask so he waited Shultz out. Shultz gave in first. "Just his head. I'm sorry to have to tell you this, sir."

From the kitchen came Calvin's angry voice, "Goddammit," and the smash of dishes in the sink. Tucker was mildly impressed that the old man's hearing was still so sharp.

Tucker answered the questioning look from the two officers.

"That's my granddad. Webb's father."

The officers nodded in sympathetic understanding. The snap and fizz of a second beer can opening filled the silence.

"Mr. McGraw, we need you to come identify the body. I know it's early—"

"I thought you said there was no body."

"Well, no sir but... I guess that's what we usually say. You're right though. Identify the head, I suppose."

"Right now?"

"Yes, sir. We can wait until you're changed, of course."

"Gimme a minute." Tucker closed the door on the cops. He passed by Milo in the hall without a word. He changed into the same jeans he wore the day before and threw some cold water across his hair to slick it down.

He stepped into the doorway of the kitchen. Calvin was on his third beer, Tucker could tell by the two empties on the counter. In the sink was a broken coffee mug and two smashed plates.

"You heard all that?"

Calvin nodded then tipped the can upside down, draining it.

"So I'll go identify him. You'll stay here?"

Calvin stared through the floor, back in time. "Fucking Stanleys."

"Yeah, we'll have to talk about that when I get back."

Tucker left his grandfather in the kitchen. Milo waited by the door, still wrapped in his sleeping bag.

"They really found just his head?"

"I guess I'll find out soon enough." Tucker nodded toward the kitchen. "Try to make sure he doesn't break anything else."

Milo nodded.

The two cops leaned against their cruiser as Tucker emerged. They each straightened up and put on their hats.

"Do I ride with you?" Tucker asked.

"You're welcome to drive yourself but we'd be happy to give you a lift."

Tucker thought about the offer for a moment. He felt in his pocket and found the keys to the Superbird. He ran a finger over the key's rough edge. "I'll drive," he said.

When he turned the key the rough gurgle of the engine seemed to him a much more satisfying sound than the thin cracking of beer can tabs.

The ritual at the police station played out with as much respect and dignity you could give a severed head. Tucker could tell the cops were thrown by the uncommon nature of the 'body'. No one would look him in the eye.

Webb's head was given a full slid-out tray in the refrigerated section of the medical examiners office. A full-length sheet covered it. The flat white sheet seemed odd with its single bump.

The coroner pulled the sheet back, careful not to look again himself and for the first time all eyes were on Tucker.

"It's him."

The head was quickly covered again.

There were questions. Who do you think could have done it? Did your father have any enemies? What did your father do for a living?

Tucker learned he was quite adept at lying. Calvin would be proud, would give credit to his genes.

When he left the station Tucker let the wheels on the car spin a bit, getting to know the full depth of the big V-8 engine.

Calvin never passed out. Not in over sixty years of drinking. You might think he was, but all you had to do was poke him or say something disparaging about Hank Williams and he'd be up and alert, if not sober.

Milo sat on the couch, dressed and gnawing on a hangnail, as Tucker walked in. Three steps in the door he heard a cascade of empty beer cans hit the linoleum floor in the kitchen.

"He's out of beer again, I think," Milo said.

Tucker peered around the corner into the kitchen where

Calvin lay face down on the kitchen table, a ruin of PBR cans at his feet. Tucker stepped up behind him and lay a hand on his shoulder. Calvin sat up fast, like a firecracker went off. He spun his head and saw Tucker. He kept staring at his grandson through slitted eyes.

"It was him," Tucker said.

"Of course it's him. Who else?"

"If you thought he was dead this whole time you sure didn't say it."

"I don't say the sky is blue every time I walk out the door, do I?"

Tucker got a Dr. Pepper from the fridge. It was, indeed, empty of beer again. "They're investigating for murder."

"Stanley."

"You think it was them?"

Calvin raised his voice. "I know it."

"How do you know it?"

"You know how many heads been found over the years in Johnson county? A bunch. An ass load. A bushel. You know how many bodies they found to go with those heads?" Calvin squinted his eyes tighter so that Tucker was convinced he couldn't see a thing. "None. Zero."

Calvin tried tilting a can to get one last drop. It came back empty. "Stanley M.O. right there. That's what you got."

"I'm going to talk to him."

"Who? Hugh?"

"Yeah."

"Not too attached to that head of yours, are you?" Calvin let out a cackling laugh and set his head down on the tabletop again.

Tucker retraced his steps to the front door, stopping by the couch in front of Milo.

"I'm dropping you back off at Mom's."

"Okay."

"I'd prefer it if you didn't tell her any of what's going on quite yet."

"Okay."

"Thanks."

Tucker opened the door and held it for Milo who picked up his overnight bag from the floor and walked outside looking to Tucker like a young boy again, a vision that had been fleeting lately.

Tucker steered the Plymouth confidently through the streets.

"Dad?" Milo said. "Grandpa's really dead, huh?"

"Yep."

"Someone killed him?"

"Seems that way."

"What are you gonna do?"

Tucker downshifted. "I have no idea."

Tucker stopped the car long enough for Milo to get out and didn't wait around to see him walk to the door. Even the slight possibility of being stopped for questioning by Jenny held absolutely zero appeal.

He made the trip across town to Hugh Stanley's office in fifteen minutes and had no more idea what he was going to say than he did when he left.

Unlike Calvin, he gave his name to the blonde receptionist and waited to be seen. The wait gave him another four minutes to think, but when the blonde told him to go in he still had nothing.

Hugh looked beyond Tucker, expecting to see Calvin. When no one else entered the room he turned to Tucker with a question on his brow.

"Where's Cal?"

"Home drunk. My dad's dead. The cops came by this morning."

"Aw, shit. I'm sorry as hell to hear that."

"All they found was his head."

Tucker studied Hugh's reaction but saw nothing. "His head?" Tucker nodded. "Damn. Webb didn't deserve that."

"My granddad seems to think that's how the Stanleys have been known to do it."

Hugh stiffened at that. "Does he now?" Tucker nodded again. "Did you tell as much to the police?"

"No. I told them a bunch of bullshit."

Hugh laid his palms flat on his desk and pursed his lips, thinking. "Headless body, huh? Or I guess the other way 'round." He let out a long sigh and slapped his open palms on the desktop. "Well, I was afraid of this. This might be Kirby."

"Your brother?"

"Yep. Things have been a bit... strained between us of late. I don't know what his beef with your dad might have been, but if anyone is following the old Stanley missing body trick it's Kirby."

Tucker swayed on his feet. He felt no sense of justice in knowing who was behind it, only more confusion. Hugh looked up from his desk as if he expected Tucker to thank him and go home. When Tucker didn't go anywhere he continued.

"I'll look into it. You know the damn cops aren't going to get anywhere. Especially if Kirby is behind it. They haven't found one of those bodies yet. Even I don't know where they

124

are. I always said they'd find Jimmy Hoffa before they found that stash of corpses."

"So what do we do?"

Hugh took on the demeanor of a loan officer who had to say no; gracious but firm.

"What do we do? We don't do anything. I said I'd look into it."

"I want to speak to him."

Hugh laughed. "You better hope your insurance is paid up. If he's so worked up and angry at the McGraws he won't care which one of you is in his sights. I'd steer clear if I was you."

Tucker clenched and unclenched his fists. Unchannelled energy raced through him. He knew Calvin would have been tearing the place apart, demanding answers and payback. An eye for an eye. A brother for a son. All Tucker could think to do was call the police, but then they'd know he lied that morning and he'd have to admit to the other illegal activity he'd played a part in over the past week.

"Tell you what," Hugh said. "That debt you owe me hardly seems fair now. Why don't you do one more job for me and we'll call it even. Pay off the note, as it were." Hugh waited for an answer. Tucker stood in quiet turmoil. "It's a drive. Up to the Canadian border. Just a pickup job though. We've got a delivery coming over and all you'd need to do is bring it back down here. Job done. You go on your merry way. What do you say?"

Tucker's inability to make any coherent decision stayed. "I'll have to get back to you."

"Sure, sure. I understand. Talk it over with Cal. Let me know by tomorrow. The delivery is being made Tuesday night."

"Okay."

"Great. And hey, listen, sorry as hell about Webb. Kirby he's... well, when he gets a notion, not much can stop it. Not sure what the hell Webb did to him, but it must have been something."

Tucker left the office feeling like he'd had his pocket picked. He'd been given the name of his father's killer and there was nothing he could do about it.

Tucker thought back ten days to when Mr. Bardsley called the office to cancel his fire insurance, the biggest tragedy of the week. The stress that phone call caused him. The loss of one policy's worth of revenue became a make or break moment. Such simple times, thought Tucker.

He sat behind the wheel of the car, the peaks and valleys of the grip providing comfort to his fingers. The bucket seat cradled him. The gearshift was sturdy when he needed it. He began to understand.

A turn of the key and the engine spoke to him.

Here were answers. Here was his father, come back to put a reassuring hand on his shoulder and tell him things would be all right.

Tucker drove home, planning. He started small. First up—a plan to get Calvin sober.

***

Hugh filled a tumbler from the wet bar across from his desk. He reached under the display bottles for the good stuff. A bottle of genuine Iowa corn hooch. Paint thinner bouquet and a rusty nail aftertaste. A man's drink. A man who could make the tough decisions.

Hugh sat back down, smoothed his tie back into place and pressed the intercom button. The blonde answered.

"Call Wyatt. Tell him he was right. I need something handled. I don't want to talk to him in case the little prick gloats."

17

Tucker sat in the dark having the argument with himself as a sort of dry run for the argument with Calvin. Trouble was, he couldn't decide on which side of the line he stood. Go or not go? Tell Stanley to fuck off or work for the men who killed his father?

There was the question of trust. Would they really cancel the debt? Would Kirby not come after them next? It sure as hell seemed like Hugh had no control over his brother. Black sheep had never come with sharper horns than Kirby Stanley. Tucker felt for all the world like he was bent over with a bright red target painted on his ass, waiting for those horns to dig in deep.

The sound of his granddad's snoring filled the house with a gentle fuzz playing out in a rhythm like the house had been transported to the beach. The thought made Tucker have to piss.

Standing over the bowl he nearly lapsed into tears for his father, but never quite made it over the edge. If there was anything so un-McGraw-like he didn't know it. To cry would be the same as riding a bicycle to work, a case of moonshine tied to the handlebars.

Tucker walked out to the couch and watched Calvin sleep. He then lay down on his own bed and had no recollection of falling asleep the next morning when he woke. He walked into the living room and found Calvin sitting up on the couch, hunched forward with spikes of his white hair gripped in his fingers.

"Morning."

Calvin grunted a greeting.

"I'll get you some coffee and as aspirin."

Calvin grunted approval.

A half hour later and two plates of eggs down the hatch, Calvin was a transformed man.

"Okay, kid, I can take it now. What did you all talk about in my absence?"

"Well, it's like this: Hugh said it was Kirby."

Calvin looked off, his mind calculating. "Hmm, that sounds about right."

"He didn't know why and he didn't exactly seem like he was gonna do anything about it."

"Hugh doesn't do anything about anything. Man might be fifteen years younger than I am, but he's older than I'll ever be."

"He offered us one last job to take care of the money we owe him."

"We don't owe him shit."

"Well, he said one more delivery and he would take the same opinion."

"What is it?"

"Pick up a delivery on the Canadian border. Drive it back here. That's it."

Calvin did more calculating. "Hmm."

"I told him I'd think about it." Tucker stared at Calvin, ready to meet his eye. "And I thought about it."

Calvin obliged and turned back to him. "And?"

"I don't want to do it."

"Why not?"

"Well, this last job almost got us killed, for one. And also if I'm not trying to find Dad then I'm through pretending to be a criminal."

"Oh, I hate to brake it to you, Tuck. You ain't pretending anymore."

"That's not true."

"So you came up with a plan to pay back the money?"

"No. But what can he do? If he comes after us, we turn in his brother for killing Dad."

Calvin rose to refill his coffee cup. "I'll ignore that based on the fact that it is so shit-all stupid it doesn't deserve a reply. And what's with this 'through trying to find your dad' bullshit? Webb got himself found. Now we have to find us a killer."

"We know who the killer is and we can't touch him."

"Says who? We take the job. It keeps us close to the Stanleys for a little while longer. Long enough to dig around and find out where Kirby is. And you know he didn't do it alone. I want anyone who had a hand in it."

Tucker narrowed his eyes a bit. "Are you sure you don't just want to do another run? I get the feeling you're enjoying this little temp job of ours."

"No more than you are," Calvin said, lifting the coffee cup to his lips. Tucker blushed a little. "I've seen the way you took to driving that car. It's bubbling up in you, Tuck. From deep down like a Texas gusher letting loose with a reserve that's been hiding for a long, long time."

"Doesn't mean I want to drive to Canada."

Calvin sat back down, leaning in close over the table. "We need their trust. I say we do the job. I say we catch us a murdering son of a bitch."

Tucker looked away then quickly brought his eyes back to Calvin's. "I'm not a criminal."

"No. You're a McGraw."

Calvin put a hand over Tucker's. His granddad's flesh felt unpolished and frayed. A life lived. Tucker felt his own hand under the sandpaper of Calvin's. Smooth. Lifeless. A hand that hadn't been places or done anything. Skin that wore gloves to chop wood, that one time he ever did chop wood. The palm covering his hand, rough from decades of shifting gears, comforted like a worn piece of fabric.

He stared into Calvin's clear blue eyes, no trace of a hangover, and said, "I'll drive."

18

Calvin made the phone call. Hugh had been cheerful about their acceptance and sympathetic to their loss. After they hung up Calvin turned to Tucker, "Glad they don't have smell-o-phones 'cause that was some serious bullshit."

Hugh had detailed the plan to drive north through Minnesota. Up around Baudette they would meet with two locals who would take them to the border. "It's not like Mexico," he assured them. "No fences and no one gives a shit."

They would meet a small truck, the Canadian drivers would get out, they would get in and come home. Simple as that.

"Easy enough," Calvin said.

"What's the hitch?" Tucker asked.

"Remains to be seen."

The meet was scheduled for midnight, the drive a solid nine hours plus. They had time for lunch before they hit the road but that was about it.

"First things first, we steal a car."

Tucker nearly dropped his ham and cheese sandwich. "What? Why?"

"We have to leave it there, don't we?"

"Why not take the orange car?"

"The Superbird is a classic. I'm not ditching it in a field so some Canadian can take it across the border and use it to drive to hockey games. That car is American and it's gonna stay in America."

Tucker found it increasingly difficult to avoid criminality in his new life as a criminal.

"We don't have time."

"Bullshit. I haven't met a car yet I couldn't steal in under two minutes. It'll be shorter than a piss break on the road."

"Fine. But get one with a heater."

"I'll do you one better and get those ass warming seats."

***

Hugh choked the neck of his corn liquor bottle in one hand and lifted the lid on the ice bucket with the other, but found only tepid water inside. He slumped his shoulders and called to the blonde.

"Erin!"

Wyatt stood by patiently, glad that he had refused a drink. That hillbilly firewater never appealed to him anyway.

"Just tell me everything is set," Hugh said.

"It is. I still don't know why we're sending them all the way to Canada when we can do it just as well right here."

"We need the delivery, don't we? And besides," Hugh gripped the lid in his hand. "Erin!" He slammed the ice bucket shut and the bottles all applauded his strength. "Having headless bodies turn up in our own backyard isn't exactly good for business."

"Bodyless heads."

"Shut the fuck up. The point is, better to do it in a pine forest eight hundred miles from here. Don't you think?"

"I guess so."

Hugh continued wringing the neck of the bottle, anxious to get inside.

"The guys, they're trustworthy?"

"Best in the business."

"That's obviously not true or they wouldn't be working out of Minnesota. What I want to know is, can they deliver the truck? You know how important this package is to us, right?"

"They can drive a goddamn truck. How hard is that?"

Hugh shook his head. "One thing I'll say about the McGraws—this thorn in my side bullshit not withstanding, they had pride in their work. You think a driver is just a driver? You've never seen an artist at work. It's the end of an era right here."

Hugh looked down at his corn hooch bottle. He thought back to the days of running cases of the stuff down out of the hills and into town. Slipping right under the noses of the cops, all with a McGraw at the wheel.

"Erin!"

***

Tucker snuck away into the bedroom for a few minutes to make a phone call. His secretary, Annabelle, had been the only other employee in the office for six years. She was dutiful and smartish and he had given over several lower level clients to her for practice. He liked mentoring and the special attention made her work all the harder.

Of course she was at her desk.

"Mr. McGraw, I was starting to worry."

"Yeah, sorry Annabelle. Look, I'm going to be a few more days. Family emergency. I need you to hold down the fort. Is that okay?"

"You've had a lot of phone calls, Mr. McGraw."

A lot for his office meant more than five, fewer than ten.

"I know you can handle it, Annabelle."

"I'll do my best. Is everything okay?"

"It's my dad's health. We've got some things to figure out."

"Oh my God. I hope he's okay."

"He'll be fine, I'm sure. I need a few more days, that's all."

"Okay Mr. McGraw. Can I call you if I have any questions?"

"Sure Annabelle. Any time."

"Thanks. You take care now. My best to your Daddy."

"Thanks."

Tucker started to doubt the intelligence of handing over his office to such a gullible girl.

"We need to stop for beer on the way out of town," Calvin said.

"Stop for—no way. Why do you need beer when we're driving?"

"You said you were driving."

"Well, maybe not the whole way. I'd like to know that's at least an option."

"A six pack then."

Before he closed the door behind them, Tucker heard voices. Urgent whispers that men used only when doing something they shouldn't. He held up a hand to stop Calvin behind him and cocked an ear like a dog. Calvin listened too.

Tucker began a slow advance around the bushes that ran along the front of his house and took the path curving right that led to the carport. He stepped on the grass patches in between the squares of concrete to keep his footsteps quiet.

Peering around the corner he saw three men grouped around the Superbird, Ambrose in the middle working a slim jim at the window.

"Just break it," whispered a cousin on Ambrose's right.

"No way, man. You know how much it costs to replace a window?"

Calvin leaned out around Tucker to see what the action was. The sandwich bag in his hand crinkled and the trio of would-be car thieves turned in unison.

Calvin dropped the bag and moved forward. "Hey! That's not your car any more."

Ambrose stayed pressed flat against the driver's side door while the two cousins stepped up to meet Calvin midway. The man on the right raised a short stick that Tucker thought he recognized as a juggling pin. Shorter than a baseball bat and fat at one end. A weapon either way you measured it.

Defenseless, Calvin surged to meet them. The club raised up and smashed down on Calvin's skull. He managed to get an arm up to block it part way, but the pop of wood against bone still sounded painful. Calvin went down.

Tucker slid forward into the car port and went for the shelf-lined walls. He grabbed for anything he could repurpose as a weapon. He lifted off the first thing his hand came across—a paint can.

He swung the gallon can on its thin wire handle and caught Ambrose across the back. The lid burst open and a thick spray of monkeyshit brown paint coated the hood of the car and

Ambrose who sunk to his knees clutching behind him at a pain he could not reach.

Both cousins advanced on Tucker and he silently thanked them for not staying and beating his granddad to death on his front lawn.

The empty can had lost its weight and therefore its usefulness so Tucker dropped it and scanned the shelves again for help. He picked up a chainsaw and spun to face his attackers who recoiled until the bright orange power cord slithered off the shelf behind him like a dead snake falling from a tree. A powerless chainsaw was about as intimidating as a bowl of pudding. Tucker threw it down to the concrete floor.

Ambrose stood and shook his arms out to throw off some of the paint. The two cousins stepped over the inert chainsaw. The one with the club took the lead.

Tucker ran his hands over the shelves, throwing glances over his shoulder as the men advanced. He reached the back wall of the carport and was penned in. On the floor beside him was a flower pot stuffed with a quarter-full bag of topsoil, a pair of dirt-caked work gloves and a set of handheld garden shears. He bent to pick up the shears.

He brandished the blades out in front of him and snapped them shut a few times in case the men forgot what garden shears did. The thin snick of the dirty blades snapping together sounded like someone clipping toenails. A snubnosed pair of scissors, that's all they were.

The cousin with the club smiled. He stepped forward, enjoying the game.

"Knock his fucking head in, Hector," Ambrose said.

Hector griped the club in his right hand and beckoned

Tucker forward with the fingers on his left. An invitation to dance.

Tucker kept snapping the shears like a baby crocodile as he moved side to side against the back wall of the carport.

"You know my cousin Tío is still in a cast from that shit you pulled on the highway," Ambrose said. Tucker figured Tío was the one who flew out of the bed of the truck. As bad as he felt for Tío, it came as good news since Tucker thought the man was dead.

"We took that car fair and square. You owed my father a debt."

"And I'll pay it. It takes a little time. But, now you're pissing me off."

Hector swung the club at the shears. The wood slapped the blades, but Tucker held on. Hector's grin grew wider.

"I'll tell you what," Tucker said. "You let me keep the car for two more days and I'll bring it back to you."

"Now?" Ambrose waved his arms out at the car like a Price is Right model. "Look at it. You ruined it."

Hector swung again. Tucker dodged and snapped the shears shut. They bit the air like a defanged cobra.

Tucker's footwork had taken him to the far wall of the carport. Boxed in again. His foot hit something and he looked down to see hedge trimmers. Same concept as the shears only bigger. He bent down and in one motion dropped the shears and came back up with the trimmer gripped in both hands.

Hector's grin faded slightly. The second cousin rounded the far side of the car, flanking Tucker's position.

Ambrose held out his hand. "Give me the keys. Maybe I can get to a car wash before this shit dries."

"Two days is all I need."

"Fuck you, man. Now it's on principal. I can't let you steal my car, fuck with me and my cousins. It don't look right, man."

Hector swung again at the air in front of Tucker and Tucker snapped back with the trimmers. They made a better sound, at least a medium sized dog. The upgrade in weapons didn't do much about the whole 3-to-1 thing.

The second cousin came closer. He moved along a set of shelves on his side and he stopped when he reached a row of jars filled with different sized nails and screws. Tucker wished he'd been on that side of the carport instead of the garden side.

A mason jar full of silver screws came sailing toward him. Tucker dipped his head and the jar bounced off his shoulder and smashed on the back wall of the carport sending hundreds of tiny screws in all directions. Hector stepped up and swung closer with the club. Tucker was too off balance to strike back with the trimmers.

Another jar, of nails this time, came at him low and fast. Tucker thrust a hip sideways to avoid the crashing jar of shrapnel and Hector lunged again.

Tucker slapped out with the trimmers, closed and non-threatening, and hit the club as it aimed for him. Hector stepped up, determined to finish the fight. Behind them Ambrose shouted something in Spanish.

Hector raised the club again and brought it down with all the force of his body weight on Tucker's left shoulder which he lifted to protect his head. The swing moved Hector off-balance and instinctively his left hand reached out to steady himself. Tucker snapped out with the trimmers like an angry bird defending its nest.

A scream filled the narrow carport and Tucker saw two

fingers arcing through the air trailed by tiny droplets of blood that seemed to be reaching to make it back inside the dark comfort of a vein.

The second cousin stood frozen with another jar of nails at the ready. Hector dropped the club and jammed his three-fingered hand under his armpit as he stepped back until he whacked his head on the high spoiler perched on the trunk of the Superbird. Finally that thing showed some use.

The second cousin threw the jar, but made the toss as a retreat maneuver the way you would hurl a rock at a grizzly bear before you ran for your life. Tucker swung the trimmers like a baseball bat and caught the jar mid-flight. The glass shattered and rained three penny nails over Tucker, marking his face and arms with dozens of tiny cuts.

Hector had turned and stumbled for the exit past Ambrose. When he hit the slick of paint on the concrete floor his feet betrayed him and he fell flat on his back, the three-fingered hand reaching out for some support, but only slamming into the rear door of the Bird, smearing the paint with blood to go along with the orange base coat and shit brown highlights.

Ambrose bent to lift his cousin, looking at Tucker like he was seeing Jason and Freddy and Michael Myers all rolled into one. Tucker stood with the blades of the trimmer open before him, a spatter of blood on top of the dirt and rust. Tiny dots of his own blood rose from the nail cuts and they gave him a crazed psychopath look.

"You fucking crazy, man," Ambrose said as he and his cousin slipped on the paint as they backed out of the carport.

Tucker heard an engine start. The second cousin had already reached the truck. He went wide around the non-paint splattered side of the car and watched as Ambrose helped his injured cousin across the lawn like file footage of Vietnam. All that was missing was the hovering helicopter and some palm trees.

Calvin was sitting up on the grass.

Tucker went to him and stuck the blades of the hedge trimmers into the lawn next to him.

"You okay?"

Calvin pulled a palm away from his head that was smeared with blood. "They got me good."

"It's alright. I got them better."

***

Twenty minutes later Calvin was cleaned up and ready to go.

Tucker hosed down the Plymouth and most of the paint came off. The seams and joints all held a new brown edging but the windshield was clear. After he put away the hose, bucket and scrub brush he took a plastic grocery bag out to the carport and picked up the fingers the way he used to pick up Pinky's shit on the lawn.

"You ought to keep those as a souvenir," Calvin said from behind him.

"Yeah, I don't think so."

"Hell of a thing. Wish I'd seen it."

"I'll paint you a picture."

Tucker dropped the bag into a green plastic garbage can and shut the lid.

19

They never did steal a car. By the time they got on the road it was getting late so they decided to take the Superbird and leave it in Minnesota. A final fuck you to Ambrose and his three-fingered cousins.

Aside from Tucker making a phone call to Milo telling him not to get any bright ideas about coming over that night—he wouldn't be home—the trip had been quiet.

He and Calvin made small talk. Calvin kept checking his map. Webb's name never came up, nor did Calvin's plans once this job was completed and their debt erased.

They passed through Bemidji about seven hours into the drive with Tucker behind the wheel for the entire run. They had entered the real 10,000 lakes part of Minnesota. They both remarked how grateful they were it wasn't winter.

Closing in on the Canadian border Tucker got tired of the small talk.

"So we do this and then what? How do we get close to Kirby?"

"Well, I figure with Hugh on our side we offer to hang

around and do a few jobs for actual money. He'll trust us and we've proven ourselves so he'll jump at the chance to get us some work."

"That doesn't get us any closer to getting the guy who killed Dad, if it was Kirby himself or someone he hired. And then what? Call the cops? What? Enough with the driving. No more jobs. Why can't you retire like everyone else your age?"

"Okay, look, I haven't thought out that far ahead yet. I'm not a big planning kind of guy. I'm used to getting an assignment and completing it. Someone else does all the logistics. I'm not a goddamn detective."

"That's obvious." Tucker shifted in his seat, the drive taking its toll on his backside.

"The thing I've learned over the years is that opportunity presents itself. And when it does you grab it. If you go looking for it then you're on a damn snipe hunt and you'll get lost in the damn woods."

"So your plan is to wait. Wait for an opportunity."

"I don't even know what you want to do. Do you want to kill Kirby for killing your dad? Do you want to send him to jail? You know damn well he wasn't the one pulling the trigger or firing up the chainsaw to separate Webb from his head, right? So do you want to find the guys who actually did it? And then what? Why don't you tell me for a change."

Tucker had no answer.

Calvin turned his attention back to the dark highway before them. "So you can see why I'm flat out stumped myself."

"Yeah. I'm sorry. I just want to be done with this. Maybe after this we should walk away."

Calvin flexed his fingers, his jaw tightening. "Yeah. Maybe we should. I didn't think I was allowed to speak that plan out loud."

"I may not have been around as many years as you but the thing I've learned is that sometimes it's best to know when you're beat. Maybe the Stanleys are untouchable. It's why they've stayed in business so long. Who are we to make them pay?"

The Plymouth's guttural V-8 sounded a little weaker. The gear change a little less musical. The road outside pointed north into blackness and dark pools of inky nothing spotted the landscape on either side of them. Never before had Calvin felt like he was driving to nowhere.

His son's death would go unpunished. He'd head back to Omaha, with no money in his pocket and no justice. The taste of the driving life had gone suddenly sour in his mouth. Even the brief visit to his glory days was tainted now.

He looked down at his map. A straight shot into Baudette. The meetup took place in an hour and a half. Perfect timing.

They'd get there and drive back the delivery under cover of darkness. Dawn would break as they passed back into Iowa, most likely. A sunrise would be a cruel joke though. Where was an eclipse to plunge the world into darkness when you needed one?

Outside Baudette the Superbird crunched into the gravel parking lot of a Gas N Save sounding like a marathon runner on the twenty-fifth mile.

Across the lot a pair of headlights flashed on and off, the Bird had been easy to spot for the car meeting them. Tucker steered the Plymouth to the far side of the lot and parked beside a mid-80s Cadillac.

Tucker put his window facing the driver of the Caddy and rolled it down for a smack in the face of late night Minnesota air. Spring or not, the bite of the far north remained.

The Cadillac window powered down and a late-30s man in a worn brown leather jacket and a high widow's peak smiled out with stained teeth. Beside him in the passenger seat was a dark-skinned black man in a black leather jacket and sunglasses. The single overhead lamp in the parking lot didn't give off enough light to attract a single moth, but this guy was protecting his eyes from the glare.

"You the guys?" the driver asked.

"I guess we are," Tucker said.

"RJ," he said about himself then threw a thumb over his shoulder to his sidekick. "Jones."

Jones lifted a hand in an imitation of a wave.

"Tucker and Calvin."

RJ got out and opened the back door to the Caddy. "We'll take you from here. Easier than having you follow us in the dark. You'll never find it."

Tucker and Calvin looked at each other, each one waiting for a last second reason from the other to back out. None came. They got out of the Superbird.

Jones was out and watching from the far side of the Cadillac. "Sweet ride. Shame to leave a beauty like that behind."

Tucker wasn't exactly sure how the man could see the car behind his shades but if any car could be seen it was the bright orange muscle car.

"It's all yours. Just don't take it to Iowa. Someone's looking for it."

"And it's not hard to find," Jones laughed.

Tucker looked back over his shoulder at the car he'd hated

so much at the start. His McGraw genes were right below the surface now, migrating closer to the top the deeper he went into the criminal life. He felt a sadness at leaving the car behind. The feeling surprised him.

He shut the door and took a last glance at the obnoxious rear spoiler, the brown paint clinging to the seams like dirt under a fingernail and he listened to the engine knocking after nearly eight solid hours of driving with stops only for gas and drive through fast food. On this trip, the Bird had eaten better than they did.

Tucker climbed in the back seat first and Calvin slid onto the big bench seat next to him.

RJ swung himself behind the wheel. "Okay boys, let's go make us some money."

20

"You don't mind me sayin', pops," RJ said as he caught Calvin's eye in the rearview, "you look like quite a vintage model for a job like this."

"I don't mind. I wear my vintage proud."

"It's just when we said we could drive this load down ourselves they said they were sending up two of the best men for it. I was kind of expecting some young hot shit guys, y'know?"

"I was hot shit and still am, son. My shit don't ever grow cold."

Jones laughed. "I like you, old timer."

"I'm glad about that, but it wouldn't make a rat's ass of difference if you hated my guts. I'm here to drive."

"Well, okay then," RJ said.

The sound of the Cadillac didn't inspire anything in Tucker. A McGraw only reacted to power and coiled aggression. The Caddy seemed all about simple transportation and a pillow of soft shock absorbers that made them feel like they were driving a waterbed.

Tucker watched the back of RJ's head, a discreet but

undeniable mullet nestled on his neck like a sleeping squirrel. Jones lit up a Tiparillo or some other kind of mini cigar. The sight allowed Tucker to finally identify the smell that permeated the upholstery. His first thought was maybe a dog had vomited in the back seat. The longer that Tiparillo burned the more he wished for the carsick dog.

They wove down unlit country lanes. Calvin studied the landscape as if trying to memorize it. Tucker saw a sign for a lakefront camping area before they turned off down a dirt drive. A chorus of frogs welcomed them to one of Minnesota's lakes.

The last cabin in a row of six fronted the water and parked next to it was a white cube truck. Bigger than a van, smaller than a semi. More or less a pickup with a metal box mounted on the back.

As soon as the Cadillac's headlight swept the truck, the doors opened and two men got out wearing heavy coats and wool knit caps.

"Thar she blows," RJ said. "The white whale."

Tucker was surprised RJ knew the reference.

The Caddy emptied of its four passengers and the six men all met in the headlight glow.

"Which one is Jones?" said one of the men in the wool caps.

Jones raised his hand. The man tossed a set of keys and Jones snatched them out of the air with precision.

Calvin pushed his hands down into the pockets on his light spring jacket.

"Any message?" Jones asked.

"Only to be careful not to fuck Mr. Parsons. Mr. Parsons don't like to be fucked. But Mr. Stanley knows this. Might be worth repeating though. Good advice never gets old."

"My granddad used to say never trust a Canadian in a wager or a fight," Calvin said. Tucker turned to him with surprise. The two men in the caps smiled. Calvin grinned, "Wanna hear a good one? A Canadian is walking down the street with a case of beer under his arm. A friend of his sees him coming and asks him, 'Hey Dave, whatcha got that case of beer for?' He says, 'I got it for my wife.' 'Wow,' says the other guy. 'Great trade.'"

The group laughed, all except Tucker.

"Good one," RJ said.

"Yeah," said the man in the wool hat. "At least we don't fuck our sisters and start foreign wars we can't win."

More laughter.

The two men turned and walked off toward the water. Jones held out the keys to Tucker. Calvin stepped between them and took the keys.

"My turn to drive."

"You boys follow us out. We'll get you back on the main highway. You driving back tonight?"

"Yep. The man says he wants it back ASAP. We oblige."

"Okay then."

Tucker heard a small outboard motor start up and the sound of a boat moving across the water headed north.

He and Calvin got in the truck.

"What was all that about?" Tucker asked.

"Giving them shit is all. Part of the game."

"I guess."

The engine turned over another uninspiring sound. Ten more hours of that yet to come.

The ride had gone from waterbed to bed of nails as the

cube truck bounced down the rutted back road away from the lake. Tucker turned down the heater which the Canadians had blowing like a blast furnace. For men who lived just south of the tundra those guys were lousy at dealing with a little spring chill.

"I always hated the long distance hauls. More than once I got the 'roids," Calvin said.

"I feel like that is a legitimate risk on this one."

"Yeah. It's not gonna be pleasant. Once we're back on solid asphalt it'll be better. These things are made for longer jaunts."

"Is it wrong if I say I kinda miss the Plymouth?"

Calvin smiled. "Not wrong at all, boy. I'll know you're human. You don't miss a car like that you probably don't cry at Sophie's Choice."

"Wait, you cried at Sophie's Choice?"

"Hell yeah. And The English Patient. And what was that one about the dog?"

"Huh." Tucker let that sink in.

Up ahead the taillights of the Cadillac swung left and became steady. Paving ahead. Calvin piloted the truck around the curve and picked up speed to match the Caddy as it coasted along in the Minnesota night.

"I tell you, it's gonna bother me until I'm in my grave that I don't know exactly what happened to Webb," Calvin said. "I still say he didn't steal that truck."

"Me too. Not a whole hell of a lot we can do about it."

"Guess I don't need to worry too much about the McGraw family reputation anymore. This is the end of the line."

"Yeah. This is our last trip."

"We shoulda brought champagne."

Calvin and Tucker smiled. Calvin watched the lights on the

Cadillac glow, wishing he had that one last drive with his son.

Up ahead the brake lights burned red on the Cadillac and RJ's arm waved out the window, ushering them to pull over.

Calvin eased the truck to the shoulder behind RJ and Jones.

"What do they want now?" Tucker said. "Exchange addresses for Christmas cards?"

"Just wrapping things up. We know the way from here."

RJ left his door open as he walked toward the truck. Jones got out and stood on his side of the Caddy, oozing smoke out of another Tiparillo.

RJ knocked on the door of the truck, but it sounded odd. Not the knock of a man's knuckles. Hard. Metallic.

Calvin rolled the window down. "We got it from here. Thanks."

"I'm afraid I'm gonna ask you boys to get out," RJ said. He lifted a gun high enough for Calvin and Tucker to see it. He waved the tip, an impatient look growing on his face.

21

Calvin opened the door slowly, showing his hands the whole way. Tucker raised his hands and began sliding across the bench seat toward the open door.

"Come on down boys," RJ said. "Got one last bit of business to do."

The truck idled loudly, nearly drowning out the frogs and crickets of the Minnesota night. Tucker followed Calvin's lead and moved slowly to stand on the shoulder. Jones had come around the Cadillac and stood by the trunk in the light of the truck's headlights, his Tiparillo glowing orange clenched between smiling teeth.

RJ waved the gun around like he forgot he had something deadly in his hand. He seemed to be remembering some speech he was supposed to make.

"Mr. Stanley thanks you for your years of service. I hereby relieve you of your duty. We'll take the truck from here."

"Why didn't you kill us back there?" Calvin asked, a contempt in his voice.

"As much as I wanted to toss you in the lake and be home before one, it's bad form to kill your workers in front of the competition. Makes us seem unstable. They might question if they were to get their money back. We can't have that."

"I see," Calvin said. His mouth stretched to a taut line. "You know, Tuck, I was really mad I missed when you kicked ass on those jackoffs down at your place." RJ bent the gun down to aim at Calvin, unsure where this monologue would go. "I'd like to return the favor though. I wish like hell I had those hedge trimmers right now."

"That's a hell of a goodbye," Jones said.

"You had to be there," Calvin shouted across the space between them. He turned back to RJ. "So are you telling me I have to spend eternity at the bottom of some nameless Minnesota lake?"

"That's pretty much it."

"Brother, that's a damn shame." Calvin clutched at his chest. He grunted like he'd stubbed his toe. "Shit!" He sank to one knee. The three other men watched him enact the telltale signs of a heart attack. "Tucker," he said through clenched teeth.

Tucker dropped his hands and stepped forward.

"Tucker," he said again. RJ crept closer as well. "My left arm."

"Well, I'll be a horny toad," RJ said.

That same left arm supposedly pulsing with pain from the stoppage in Calvin's heart shot out and clamped down over the pistol in RJ's hand.

Calvin spun the wrist around and fired a shot into RJ's hip using his own finger to do it. RJ howled and bent. Calvin stayed on one knee, keeping RJ between him and Jones. He turned his head to Tucker.

"Kill the lights."

Tucker squat walked back to the truck as Jones' first shot rang out. Jones sidestepped along the soft shoulder, retreating backward along the driver's side of the Cadillac as he fired blind. Literally blind with his sunglasses still on.

Calvin wedged a finger into the trigger of the pistol and fired again, this time into RJ's gut. He let go of the pistol and fell flat to the ground. On cue the lights on the truck went dark. Jones fired twice more but hit nothing.

The frogs went quiet. Calvin looked up from his position on the ground, brought the gun up and fired at the tiny dot of orange glowing up ahead.

A choked off yell sounded and the orange dot went dead. The sound of Jones's body falling to the gravel of the shoulder reached Calvin and Tucker as a puff of dust caught the Cadillac's headlights. Calvin slipped forward and hugged his back against the Caddy. Near the back bumper he looked down the length of the car to see Jones' body laid out near the front tire. Steam rose from the open head wound.

Calvin turned and stood straight, facing the truck.

"Turn 'em back on."

Tucker obliged. RJ writhed in the dirt under the spotlight of the truck's glare. The engine in idle covered most of his scratching in the dirt. Calvin stood over him, gun at the ready.

"Stanley put you up to this?"

RJ's face tightened as he grimaced. He seemed to be willing his teeth to clench harder, his eyes to shut tighter in some futile attempt to make the pain go away.

He managed, "Yeah. Stanley."

"For that bit of honesty I won't kill you. Start walkin'."

RJ's eyes flew open. Calvin inferred the question, What the fuck are you talking about?

"Start walking, I said. Now."

RJ rolled over on one side keeping a hand over his bleeding gut. It took several attempts to stand and Calvin didn't help at all. Tucker watched from inside the truck like the scene before him was a little play in the bright spotlight of headlamps.

Calvin pointed with the barrel of the gun. "Go on."

RJ knew better than to stand around and question it. He limped off in the direction Calvin pointed and only a few feet off the shoulder they could hear him splash into shallow water. The sloshing water sounds mixed with the sucking noises of his feet slurping in and out of the mud as RJ made his way across lake #10,001.

Calvin watched him go for a minute then stepped up into the cab of the truck.

"Not exactly chopped off fingers, but it'll do."

Tucker was more than happy to be a spectator. "Jesus Christ, that was close."

"Sure was." Calvin handed Tucker the gun. He put it in the glove box as Calvin dropped the white truck into gear and began to pull out.

"Wait," Tucker said. Calvin stopped the truck. "Keys."

Tucker dropped down out of the truck and walked over to the Cadillac. He stepped across Jones' body, careful not to look down, and reached inside to take the keys from the Caddy. He left the lights on.

He straightened and stepped away from Jones before hurling the key ring out into the black water. Over the truck's urgent engine he never heard them splash.

**

155

"Two words come to mind—cluster and fuck." Calvin sped south on 72 passing signs for the Red Lake Indian Reservation.

"Did that really happen?" Tucker asked.

"Sure as shit did. It happened and then some."

A gas station glowed ahead, a beacon in the blackness around them. Tucker had started to feel there wasn't a blacker state in the union than Minnesota. A gust of wind shook the truck like the whole state was elbowing them in the ribs to get the hell out.

Calvin stopped anyway.

He eased the truck into the lot away from the pumps and out of the circle of yellow light that haloed down from a high pole. He shut off the engine and they both sat in the stillness, trying to let the quiet fill their lungs.

Calvin broke the silence. "So Stanley tried to kill us."

"Looks like it. But which one? Kirby or Hugh?"

"Does it matter?"

"Kind of. We made a deal with Hugh. If we deliver the truck to him maybe he can call off his brother."

"Ain't no calling off a rabid dog."

"So what do we do?"

Calvin kept his hands on the wheel, staring out into the trees looking for answers. His stomach made a loud gurgling sound both men ignored.

"I'm gonna look at it."

"At what?"

"The cargo."

Tucker watched the profile of his granddad's face. "I thought that wasn't allowed."

"Yeah, well, all bets are off, I say." Calvin opened the door and a gust of night air filled the cab. Tucker slid out of his side and they both walked to the back of the truck. Tucker checked the parking lot for anyone watching, but there were no signs of life.

Calvin paused with his hand over the latch to the roll door. He was about to break a hundred years of protocol no McGraw had ever broken. The decision required a moment's thought. A moment was all he gave.

The door rolled up and both men squinted in the dim light to see inside the cube. A dozen banker's boxes were stacked neatly and lashed down so they wouldn't move. The load would have fit in a regular van so there was space enough to move a friend's couch if they called and throw in an unused treadmill while you were at it.

The boxes were unmarked. Tucker studied Calvin's face but saw only puzzlement. The breeze made a hollow sound against the open hole of the door, the kind of sound an empty mineshaft might make. Calvin gripped one of the chrome handholds and hoisted himself inside the cargo space. Tucker stayed behind.

Calvin lifted the lid on the topmost box and peered in.

Tucker stood on his tiptoes to get a look, but it was pointless.

Calvin continued to stare into the box. He opened the one next to it, and the one next to that until the top row of four boxes stood lidless.

"Tuck," Calvin said. "You know when I was saying about seeing an opportunity and taking it?"

Tucker didn't know where this was headed. "Yeah."

"Well, this here is opportunity presenting itself."

He lifted a small bundle from a box and held it up for Tucker to see. It took his eyes a moment to register what the object was. A small stack of money wrapped with a loop of bank paper denoting the denomination, which Tucker couldn't read.

Calvin tapped a foot against the bottom row of boxes confirming that they weren't empty.

"Get up here and help me count this."

22

12 million in cash.

They each struggled to figure why the Stanleys would move that much cash down from Canada, but the why didn't change the situation.

"Laundered. That's what I figure," Calvin said. The coffee at the truck stop was strong—trucker grade diesel—and the eggs smelled like heaven. They'd stopped south of Minneapolis once they felt like they'd hit civilization proper. Tucker couldn't stop throwing glances out the window to the truck, feeling certain he would see somebody come along and slim jim the door and take off with it at any second.

Their booth was two seats away from the nearest person but Calvin kept his voice low. "They send the profits up north, mix it around, change for those funny dollars and back again and bingo—it comes back clean as they day it was minted."

"You think so?"

"Best I got right now."

"So what do we do with it?" Tucker ignored his coffee. More jitters was not what he needed.

"What we got out in the truck are twelve million little

159

bargaining chips. That bastard wanted us dead. Now we got the best thing in the world—leverage."

"So what do we do?"

"I tell you what we don't do. We don't give it back to them right away. We find out the truth behind Webb's murder. Then we get a few promises, then we take our share and get out of Dodge."

"Where to? Omaha?"

"You could do worse."

"What about Milo?"

"Send him a check. Look, this changes things. Twelve million is a hell of a lot of money. Not to mention the two bodies we left behind up there."

"Only one body."

"Tucker, if you think that boy is ever coming out of that water again you're dumber than I thought." Calvin took another sip of coffee.

Tucker turned his eyes down to the chipped Formica table. He pressed his fingertip over individual sugar crystals spilled there, picking them up and then brushing them off.

"So, what, we drive up to Hugh Stanley's office and start making demands?"

Calvin put his mug down with a clank. "I ain't worked out the details yet. If you've got any suggestions I'm open to hearing them."

Tucker continued pressing sugar crystals in the grooves of his fingerprints. "We could run." Calvin pinched his eyebrows together, confused. "Just take the money and go. Twelve million, I could get Milo and split. We could get lost with that much. I could pay off Jenny."

"That's flat out stealing."

"At this point..."

Calvin raised his coffee mug in a toast. "Told you you weren't pretending anymore." He slurped down the black brew with a smile.

Crossing the line into Iowa was more welcome than Tucker ever thought possible. Calvin had made his case for trying to get information out of Stanley over the phone and if that didn't work they would run. Seemed like a decent compromise. At least it put off the moment when Tucker went from bystander and witness to perpetrator of a multimillion dollar heist.

"Of course it could all go bad," Calvin said.

"Yeah," Tucker smirked. "Could go bad. Right."

"I mean the law. Jail time. Stanley will kill us. Sheriff will put us away. Won't be as bad for me. A life sentence isn't all that much. For you..."

"Jesus Christ." Tucker started out the window resting his chin on his hand, the vibration of the truck coming up through his elbow sitting on the armrest. Every rut in the road rattled his teeth. A single light glowed over the door to a silo in the distance. Farm work, thought Tucker. Simple. You got up, fed the cows, tended to the crops. You didn't talk to anyone. The only car you drove was a tractor. Born surrounded by farms on all sides and he blew the chance to pick the simple life.

If they did run, the thing he looked forward to more than anything was changing his name.

"I did time, you know." Calvin let that hang in the air.

"I didn't know."

"1948. For six months. Labor camp. Wasn't easy." Tucker had nothing to add to the story so he sat and listened. "I went in thinking it would be fun and games. Surrounded by friends, or at least people of a similar element. Warden was a bastard. Guards were bastards. Most of the inmates were bastards. Guys got in there and it's like they didn't give a fuck anymore. They gave up on humanity for their stretch. Warden ran a tight ship, but when their backs were turned it was a fucking jungle."

They left highway 35 and merged onto the 20, closer to home.

"I saw a guy stab another guy in the neck with a fork at mealtime. The fork still had mashed potatoes on it. He jabbed him twice real quick and then kept on eating. Potatoes had blood all over them like gravy. Caught the guy right in the artery. Some kind of wizard with that fork, knew exactly where to strike. I thought we were all on the same side in there. That's when I learned that it's every man for himself when the going gets tough."

"I'd say the going is pretty tough for us right now."

"So you get my point."

"I think I do."

"We got something Stanley wants. Something he needs. He's hurting for money. He'll play ball. I bet for twelve mil, he'll give us his own brother. My boy—your Daddy— he needs some justice right about now."

The unmistakable smell of a hog farm swept through the cab. Smelled like home.

23

By the time they made the final turn for home light spread wide over the brown fields of dirt, spring seeds still asleep under soft manure blankets. When the sun rose Tucker finally felt sleepy. The steady buzz of *what the hell do we do now?* had kept him awake for the drive home, but the night was reaching out over the hours to drag him back to tired.

There had been much discussion of where to end up, what Hugh might have known, if the bodies were found yet. Was Hugh expecting a phone call after the deed was done? Was the call going direct to Kirby? Either way the two men decided a neutral place was a better choice so they drove to Webb's house.

The lawn had the equivalent of a five o'clock shadow and the house overall had the look of a hangover with shutters.

The cube truck wouldn't fit in the garage. Both men got out and stared at the right angles of the truck, their sleep-deprived brains unable to process the new wrinkle in the plan.

"Maybe let the air out of the tires?" suggested Tucker.

"Naw, it's got a good three feet on the top of that door."

They split up and each surveyed a side of the house. On

Tucker's side a tree stood on the spit of lawn leading to the backyard. They met again on the front lawn and Calvin gave his assessment.

"I can make it."

Tucker stayed outside and gave directions with hand motions as Calvin guided the truck slowly through the high grass to the wider expanse of the backyard. Tucker braced for a neighbor to look out his window and see the cargo truck passing by three feet from his kitchen window and meeting them out back with a shotgun and a phone call to the cops, but either the family next door were heavy sleepers or they all had a few too many the night before.

Tucker ran ahead and moved several lawn chairs that were coated with dead leaves and held pools of rusty water in the seats. Calvin guided the truck to the center of the lawn and parked it at a slight angle like a display at an auto show.

Tucker walked to the back door, moved aside a flower pot filled with nothing but dirt and retrieved a spare key. They walked through the sliding glass door into the kitchen at the back of the house, their ears ringing with the phantom sounds of the truck's engine.

"Dad?"

Both of them spun. Tucker thought they'd caught a burglar, Calvin thinking he'd found a ghost.

Milo stood in the doorway of the kitchen. Tucker let his shoulders sag, his muscles untense from their high alert.

"What the hell are you doing here?"

"You said I couldn't go to your place so..."

Calvin went to the fridge to search out a beer.

"Why aren't you at your mom's?"

"I told you, Dad. It sucks there."

164

Tucker put both palms down on the counter, too tired to argue. Calvin twisted the cap off a long neck bottle of Milwaukee brew.

"It's good. He can help us unload it." Beer foam gathered at the corners of Calvin's mouth.

Tucker tried to shoot him a withering stare but his tired face was shooting blanks.

"Unload what?" Milo asked.

"Just some boxes," Tucker said. "We need to get them into the garage for safekeeping."

"Okay. I can help."

"Great." Calvin tipped the bottle and drained the rest.

Tucker could feel the question on Milo's mind but the boy never asked it. One box each for four trips and all twelve banker's boxes were piled neatly in the garage behind Webb's old 1970 Buick GSX with two thick black stripes running down the middle of the hornet-yellow body. The two car garage was filled out with an old Barracuda and Webb's '69 Camaro Z28 sat out front under a car cover, bird shit not welcome.

The men went inside.

"I'm gonna make a phone call," Calvin said.

Tucker turned to Milo. "Can you give us a minute?"

"Yeah, sure." The boy moved off down the hall to get dressed, the mystery of his dad's secretive life becoming a new normal.

Calvin dialed Hugh Stanley's office from a wall-mounted phone in the kitchen. He knew no one would be there.

"Hugh," he spoke into the answering machine. "You know who this is. And you know your boys up there didn't do such a hot job of taking us out. If you're looking for them, have someone drag the lakes and eventually you'll find them." Tucker sat at a stool against the bar-height countertop that overlooked the breakfast nook. Calvin stared at the floor as he spoke. "We have your money, you son of a bitch. And that's right, I looked. Bet you didn't expect that. It's a lot of green and I expect you'll be needing it back. All we want is the man who killed my son. Even trade. And then you get out of our lives for good. Our two families have been tangled together like snakes at an orgy for too fucking long. Time to go our separate ways. We'll be in touch."

He hung up the phone and left his hand resting on the wall-mount. "Well, can't get that genie back in the bottle."

"I need sleep," Tucker said.

"Yeah."

Both men slumped off like zombies to pass out cold.

Six hours later Tucker bolted upright, thinking of Jenny. He took a moment to look around him. The room seemed unfamiliar and yet he knew he'd been there before. He remembered where he was and it dawned on him that he was laying in his childhood bedroom.

He threw off the sheets and walked down the hall, following the sound of a TV. Milo sat on the couch watching MTV. Tucker could remember when they played music on that channel.

"Where's Granddad?"

"Still asleep. It's almost two o'clock."

"Where?"

"In the master bedroom."

Tucker found Calvin spread out on Webb's old bed, a

steady snore in the air. He almost woke him to tell him what he'd thought—that Jenny was perhaps in danger. That they had come after him when Webb pissed the Stanleys off, they were just as likely to come after the rest of the family. He let Calvin sleep.

Tucker called Jenny from the kitchen phone. There was no answer.

He went back to the living room. "Milo? Is your mom at the store today?"

"I guess so. Why?"

"I need to reach her."

"Shit, Dad, are you gonna tell her I'm here?"

Tucker ignored the profanity. "Yes, but that's not why I need to reach her. What's the number at the store?"

"I don't know. It's on speed dial at home."

Tucker walked to the front door. On the wall inside the entry was a large wooden board cut on a jigsaw to look like a key with four tiny hooks embedded in it. A key ring hung from three of the four hooks. Webb was nothing if not fastidious about his cars and he kept the appropriate logo on each ring. Tucker passed a finger over a round Buick logo, a Plymouth logo and finally a gold and blue Chevy logo. He lifted the keys and went outside.

The roar of the Camaro's engine sounded like a welcome call to an old friend and the gearshift in his hand greeted him with a handshake.

24

Even through the nastiest, most kick-in-the-balls painful times of the divorce, Tucker never wished any harm to Jenny. He knew guys who talked openly, if facetiously, of hitting an ex in the face with an axe, but he only ever wanted Jenny to be happy with or without him. Preferably with.

After a lifetime of shifting gears to accelerate away from his family and his name he found a quiet slow-lane life with Jenny and Milo, their little sidecar.

As he rolled up on her shop, Little Big Kids, a store for 4-10 year-olds, he thought about asking Jenny to go for a ride in the Camaro. Webb had been telling him for thirty years that chicks dug cars and he'd never listened.

The front of the store was empty of people. Mannequin kids modeled new styles that reminded Tucker of hookers from the 80s. The requisite University of Iowa gear occupied one corner with Herky the Hawk flapping his wings to victory on sweatshirts, T-shirts, pants and backpacks. Around there it would be hard to get a business license if you weren't selling at least something with Herky on it.

Jenny not sitting behind the cash register wasn't unusual. It was midday and the door set off a digital bell in the back room if someone came in. She'd be out in a second and Tucker would have to endure the look of crushing disappointment on her face when she saw he wasn't a paying customer and then endure a lecture-meets-WWE smackdown about Milo.

Jenny did not appear. Tucker heard voices from the back. He stepped close to the door leading to the office and storeroom.

Peering around the corner he saw Jenny flanked by two men in dark suits with their backs to him. The conversation seemed civil enough, still he tensed.

Between her two gentleman callers she spotted him.

"You!" She stood and split the men as she charged forward. "Now you got the cops looking for you?"

And not beat cops. Detectives in suits. Shit. He looked them up and down for signs of Minnesota. They looked more Ozark Mountains.

Jenny stood under his nose as he kept eyes on the two men slowly turning in his direction. "You piece of shit. What did you do with him? You're lucky I didn't call the cops myself. This is fucking kidnapping is what it is."

"Jenny, calm down."

"I can't find Milo. The cops can't find you. I told them. I told them you have our son and that is a direct violation of our divorce agreement. You'll never see him again, Tucker. Never."

The cop with the crew cut stepped up. His partner with the heavy brows and a tattoo peeking out from under his collar let his buddy do the talking.

"Mr. McGraw, we've been looking for you. Is your grandfather with you? Waiting in the car, maybe?"

"I'm alone."

"Fair enough. Maybe you can take us to him. We'd really like to talk to you both."

Jenny was emboldened by her new friends. "You better fucking tell me where Milo is before they take you away and lock you up. What the hell have you been doing with that old man anyhow? Did you get our son involved?"

"Milo's fine, Jen. Everything is fine."

"Mr. McGraw, you'll have to come with us now."

Tucker looked into the eyes of the men who would change his life. He couldn't argue. He'd been fighting himself for the things he'd done. He wasn't about to start justifying the crimes he'd been a part of because he was trying to find his dad, and later his dad's killer. Wrong was wrong.

The man with the thick brows lowered them to an intimidating level. His hand remained at his side. No cuffs came out. No rights were read. Tucker had shown no signs of resisting, but the men's actions, or inaction, gave him a moment's pause.

"Jenny, did you see these guys badges?"

"What? No. They aren't here to arrest me. They were looking for you, jackass."

"I know that," Tucker inched a half step backward. Crew Cut matched him in the slow movements of hunters not wanting to disturb prey. "But, Jenny... these aren't cops."

She turned to them, a betrayed but confused look on her face. "Huh?"

Tucker reached out to a silver rolling rack empty of clothes but hung with two dozen wooden hangers. He clamped a hand around a hanger while Crew Cut shoved Jenny aside as he charged. Eyebrows reached into his pocket and pulled out a short black stick about the size of a thick chopstick. He flicked his wrist and it unfolded end over end like a magic trick until it became a stick of some danger.

Tucker arced his arm out in a wide half moon, the hanger clenched in his fist with the metal question mark jutting between his middle and ring finger like he was Captain Hook chasing after Peter Pan. The hook caught Crew Cut across the cheek like a widemouth bass and hooked him good.

Tucker tugged the man's head, setting the hook and ripping the hanger from Tucker's hand. By sheer instinct, the base desire to get the hurt away from you as quickly as possible, Crew Cut reached up and yanked down on the hanger, tearing a perforation in his cheek before he even knew he'd done it.

Eyebrow's magic stick came across Tuckers shoulder blades like a metal switch grandma used to use to cane your shins when you made her mad. She would have liked one of those compact metal jobs, though half the fun for her was making the kids get their own switch for her to beat them with.

Tucker bent at the knees, but stayed off the ground. Jenny screamed and backed into a cork board tacked up with employee schedules, state safety rules, take out menus and a few cut out comic strips about customer complaints.

As Eyebrows readied another blow, Tucker swung a child-size mannequin into his arms and spun, holding the toddler out in front of him to take the punishment. The cane came crashing down again and the blank-faced body form lost an arm.

Tucker threw the rest of the body at Eyebrows. He turned to run, but slipped in a pool of blood Crew Cut had spit onto the floor. The injured man writhed around with both hands at his cheek, but the blood ran around his fingers and stained Jenny's laminate wood flooring.

"Jenny, let's go," Tucker called.

"Who are they?"

"Just come on." Tucker extended a hand to her and she reached for it. Like God and Adam on the Sistine Chapel they were a fingerprint apart when the cane swung down again. The metal caught Jenny's hand and she squealed as her arm was thrust down and out of Tucker's grasp.

Tucker reached behind him and plucked a thumbtack off the cork board, secretly wishing Jenny had opened a chainsaw, machete and crowbar emporium. Perhaps a nail gun test center or an indoor archery range.

Tucker pushed forward, kicking away Crew Cut's legs to get closer to Eyebrows and slap a left hand on the wrist above the cane. He jabbed the thumbtack straight out as if he had a very urgent child's drawing of a lopsided fire truck to hang on the wall. The tiny point of the tack pierced Eyebrow's cheek and he yelped like a kicked poodle.

Keeping a grip on the wrist, Tucker poked and poked and poked the tack in a mosaic pattern all across the man's face. Eyebrows would turn his head only to get a hot pinpoint of pain on one cheek, then swivel away to get a bee sting under his eye.

Ten, twelve, fifteen, twenty pokes and the man's face looked like an overripe strawberry leaking juice.

Jenny, either to stop Tucker's death by a thousand cuts or for some other inner bravery she'd found, swung a 3-hole punch into Eyebrow's face. His hand went slack and he dropped the magic stick.

Tucker reached out to Jenny and this time they connected.

"We have to call the police," she said.

"No cops."

He pulled her along toward the door, but found himself tilting toward the floor. Crew Cut had tangled his legs around Tucker's and now they were both flat and flailing. Crew Cut pulled his hands away from his face and the crazed blood stained carnival look of his face made Tucker recoil. The wounded man started crawling towards Tucker in an image that would haunt his dreams for years to come. A long line of blood and saliva sagged from the gash in his cheek. The cut was irregular, not knife-like clean, but torn like the edge of an old treasure map.

Tucker rolled on his back and started kicking out with his feet like he'd learned to fight in a women's self-defense workshop. Crew Cut's blood-slick hands tried to latch on to Tucker's Nikes, but his feet were moving too fast and more kicks than not were landing.

Jenny brought the 3-hole punch down on the top of the crew cut, but he kept on the attack. She whacked him once more and dropped the hole punch and leaped over the two men grappling on the ground and bolted out the back room into the store, leaving Tucker behind.

She'd left him two against one. For the first time he wished her a tiny bit of harm. Maybe one jab with the thumbtack.

Eyebrows was up. His face dripped beads of blood like he was sweating the stuff. Tucker kicked for his life but Crew Cut grabbed hold of his ankles. Can't drive your way out of this one, Tucker thought.

"Get out." Her tone was firm and rehearsed. Somehow familiar. Tucker had heard those words from that voice before. Maybe not with quite as much anger, but close.

"Get out both of you."

That was new.

The kicking stopped. Crew Cut's grip loosened. Eyebrow's advance halted. Tucker looked over his shoulder and up to see Jenny standing in the doorway, legs shoulder width apart, arms out in front of her with elbows locked and a dull black .38 in her hand. The store security system.

She looked like a recruiting poster for the local police.

"Get the fuck out of my store or I start shooting off dicks."

Eyebrow started backing up. Crew Cut pushed up on formerly blood-slick, now blood-sticky hands. His breath sucked wet and uneven from the new ventilation in his face.

Jenny stood firm and the nose of that gun didn't shake one bit as she watched them all the way out the back door.

Tucker thought she'd have a lot more to say to the two men. She always was quick with an insult or a threat for him. Instead she waited until the back door clicked shut before exhaling loudly and letting her body fall like that breath of air was all that held it up.

Tucker sat up. "You need to come with me and I'll explain."

Tears welled in her eyes. Tucker stood. "I promise. Come with me. Milo's there too."

He took the gun from her and she let herself be led from the store. She locked all the doors and set the alarm. She pulled down the metal roll door over the front of the store which she hadn't done in years except for the odd tornado warning.

Tucker opened the door to the Camaro and she got in. If she was even vaguely impressed by the car she didn't show it.

25

Tucker explained as best he could which still left Jenny with more questions than she could organize in her brain, so she sat silently while they all crowded the door between her frontal lobe and her tongue.

Calvin sat on a chair he'd pulled into the living room from the kitchen. No way he was sitting on the same couch with that woman. Milo had been banished to the back bedroom to await the all clear from his dad.

"Does it make a bit of sense?" Tucker asked.

"Not a whole lot. Should I be scared?"

Calvin spoke up for the first time since he grunted a hello when she arrived. "If they're trying to kill us, and that was before we stole the money, you can be sure they don't have the best of intentions with you." He sipped on the beer he'd been nursing all through Tucker's recounting of events. Thankfully the boy had left out any exact dollar amounts on the truck's contents, calling it only, "A lot of money."

Jenny regarded the old man as if he sat in the living room wearing full Klan robes holding a burning flag in his hands while kicking a dog and pissing on a picture of Ronald Reagan shaking hands with Jesus. "I might have known you were at the root of all this."

Calvin chuckled.

"Oh, it's funny, is it?" Jenny went into full attack mode. "My ex-husband you can keep, but you got my son involved in this, you piece of shit. Some century old family argument and now my only child is in danger of being killed by some drug gang? Who do you think you are?"

Calvin raised his beer can in a toast. "Calvin McGraw, ma'am. I'm an outlaw." He tipped back and finished the can.

Jenny let out a frustrated grunt and crossed her arms over her as she sat back into the couch.

"Don't blame him," Tucker said. "You can blame me. I let my principals run a little loose when I thought I was going to find out where my dad was. I got a little, I don't know what. Tunnel vision I guess. I think I started down the road when I was still in shock from the visit I got from Stanley's men. I should have taken some time to step back and think it through. I never invited Milo into this, though. He kept showing up on his own."

"At which point you should have brought him straight back home."

"You're right. I let my feelings about our situation put him in danger. I'm sorry."

"Don't apologize to her," Calvin said.

"Granddad, why don't you head off to bed. Jenny and I got a lot of talking yet to do."

"I'm not tired."

"Then take the rest of your beers and go watch TV or something. You're not helping right now."

Calvin stood from his chair like an angry teenager and

176

stomped out of the room.

"Charming as ever," Jenny said.

"Give him a break. His son did die, y'know."

"And your dad." Jenny softened now that Calvin had left the room. She turned to Tucker, laid a hand on his arm. "I am sorry about that. He was a good man."

"You called him a son of a bitch on our wedding day." A grin tugged at the corner of his mouth.

"He was both, if you can be that. Either way I'm sorry."

"Thanks."

Tucker couldn't be sure, but he thought he felt a crack in the ice between them.

Calvin stacked three empty beer cans into a tower then slowly pushed them over with a finger. That woman being in the house sent shivers up his spine. He knew now what is was to lose a son. Tucker's boy hadn't died, but that woman took him away from his father.

The McGraw men's curious habit of having only children, all of them blessedly boys, made each child special—and vulnerable. Those damn Stanleys bred like rabbits.

Even Jenny and Tucker talking over God knows what in the next room couldn't distract his mind for long from the thought of what came next. No word yet from Hugh. They obviously were not going to give in easily. Going after the family, even the estranged family, showed their commitment to causing harm to anyone they felt slighted them.

Those twelve boxes provided insurance and also a lure with the same pungent stench of catfish bait. They could wait it out at Webb's place for a while, but sooner or later the fight was going to come to them, or they would have to bring it to the Stanleys.

"So when we were married, I bet you didn't think I was capable of all this."

"Inciting a gang of drug dealers to try to kill you? No. That was not at all on the radar." She smiled. Actually smiled in the same room with Tucker. He tried not to let himself think it was just the wine.

"How about this?" Tucker leaned over like a senior on prom night and pushed his lips onto hers. Jenny didn't know what to do. She let the kiss happen. She didn't exactly give it back, but she didn't push him away.

Tucker stayed there, his body covering hers on the couch. He could feel his armpits becoming moist as the stress of holding that kiss drained all the blood from his face. He broke away and took his seat again, watching her eyes for anger or desire and wondering if he was going to be able to tell the difference.

Jenny slowly opened her eyes. She said nothing. She didn't move. Memories of their marriage played in her mind.

Tucker got tired of waiting and leaned forward again. If he was going to go so far as to steal twelve million dollars he might as well kiss a girl who once loved him.

This time she kissed back.

The wine on her tongue made him feel even more like a drunk teenager. Just like riding a bike he knew her movements, he knew when to pivot his head, when to pause and when to push his mouth harder onto hers.

Jenny broke the clinch. She gently lifted Tucker off her, not shoving him away but letting him know the moment had passed.

"I can't."

"Roy?" He asked.

"Ron," she said. "This is too confusing right now."

"Sorry."

"No it's... it's okay. I can't. Not right now."

"I understand. You're right. Goodnight."

Tucker pulled the blanket down from the back of the couch before he left and covered her. She smiled at him but her heart wasn't in it.

Tucker went back to share a bed with Milo and dream of possibilities.

Calvin lay awake in bed thinking over a few possibilities of his own.

Possibility 1: Take the money and get the hell out of town. And not back to Omaha.

Possibility 2: Drive the truck right up Hugh Stanley's ass and go out in a blaze of glory.

Possibility 3: Give Tucker the money and go see Hugh alone. If he got at least some McGraw blood maybe the old bastard would be satisfied enough not to search for Tucker.

Possibility 4: A car load of Stanley men were on their way over at that very second to kill him and everything in the house that moved.

Calvin thought that last possibility would be the one to stay on the table for the rest of his life if they didn't sort this mess out. He still believed Hugh would want the money back bad enough to give up Webb's killer. Stanley had sold a lot more for a lot less over the years.

He spun the empty plastic rings from his six pack around a finger. He hadn't ingested nearly enough beer to make sleep happen yet.

***

Tucker woke up in the strange bed. He took a moment to remember he wasn't in his own house. He looked to his left and saw Milo sleeping the sleep of the teenager—intense and coma-like. Light crept in around the edges of the curtains like the sun had crash landed in the backyard overnight.

Tucker eased out of bed without waking Milo. The clock read 10:13.

He walked down the hall, bare feet padding on the wood floors, creaking the same board that had creaked since the early 80's. He peered slowly over the top of the couch to see if Jenny was still asleep, but the couch was empty and the blanket folded over the back cushion.

Tucker went to the kitchen and found Calvin eating a bowl of cereal at the round, chrome-legged table. Tucker listened for the sound of the shower running down the hall. There was only the sound of Calvin slurping milk between crunches of wheat flakes.

"Where's Jenny?"

Calvin slurped in another mouthful. "Gone," he said through the cereal.

"Gone? What do you mean?"

He swallowed. "I mean she's gone. Gone for good. Left town by now I suspect. 'Least that's what she said she was gonna do."

"Back up. What are you talking about?"

Calvin stood and brought his bowl to the sink and placed it there with a ringing ceramic tone. "Just what I said. She's

180

gone for good."

"When?"

"Last night."

"You saw her?"

"Yep."

A raw hurt played over Tucker's face, like he was holding fire but helpless to let it go.

"Can you stop being so goddamn coy and explain what the hell happened?"

"I got up to get more beer. She was laying there in the dark crying. I couldn't just ignore it. I had to pass right by the couch to get in here. We talked a bit and she seemed real confused so I made it easy on her."

The hurt was coalescing into anger now. "How?"

"I gave her some money and told her she could go."

"How much money?"

"A box."

"A million bucks?" Calvin nodded. "What the hell did you do that for?"

"To see if she would take it. And Tucker, you know what happened? She took it like I knew she would and she left. She left you. She left Milo. She saw a million bucks and she ran. She's exactly the woman I knew she was."

Tucker began pacing the floor, his bare feet slapping the linoleum.

"Did you scare her? Did you tell her more stories about how she was in danger?"

"She was in danger. You know she was. Why the hell do you think you got on your white horse and went after her yesterday? Don't take this out on me. I did you a favor."

"Oh, bullshit. You hated her and you chased her off."

"I didn't chase nothing. You should have seen her eyes when I opened that box. Cartoon dollar signs lit up."

Tucker spun and moved quickly back to the bedroom. Milo slowly eased out of his fog as Tucker dressed noisily.

"What's up, Dad?"

"Nothing. Go back to sleep."

Out by the front door Tucker called out to Calvin. "Where are the keys?"

"She took 'em."

"What?"

"I gave her the Camaro too."

"Jesus Christ." Tucker scanned the hook and took down the Buick key ring.

He sped away from the house leaving a half dozen banker's boxes exposed in the garage.

26

Tucker left the car idling next to the curb. He banged twice more on the door to Jenny's house even after he knew she wasn't there. He sat on the concrete porch steps and stared at his shoes for a long while. Still exhausted, now dazed, time ground to a slow ooze. Finally he got up and went back to the car.

A short ride later he found that the store was locked, the CLOSED sign tilted at an angle in the front window.

Tucker got back in the car and sat. What would he tell his son? Or, Christ, what was Calvin telling him right at that moment?

He couldn't help thinking he drove her away with that stupid kiss. Did she hate him that much she had to run? Or was he worth a price to forget and Calvin found it. One million dollars.

He snapped back to the present, unsure how long he'd been drifting in the past, replaying his entire relationship all the way from first meeting until last night. But now that he was back, the rest of that money called to him like a homing beacon. There would be time enough to mourn Jenny, but getting that money out of his life and meeting his father's killer face to face was a more pressing issue.

He steered the Buick by his own house to gather some clothes. Right away he knew something was wrong.

Burnt-out road flares were scattered in the street leading up to his house like discarded cigars with long trails of ash. A strip of yellow caution tape had come untied and waved in the wind like a long tendril of seaweed under the water.

He parked across the street. His driveway was blocked by another strip of bright yellow tape. If the flares were stubbed out smokes his house was the whole ashtray. Black except for the gray wisps of smoke still curling from some heat buried deep under the remnants of his home. Charred beams marked the four corners of the foundation and the chimney stood tall, the bricks blackened by the fire. Shapeless blobs he guessed were his furniture squatted inside the crumbling charcoal husk of his house.

Tucker stood on the lawn and stared. The smell burned into his brain replacing any childhood memories of campfires or night before Christmas marshmallow roasts.

"Tucker? Jesus, is that you?"

He turned to see Bill, his next door neighbor, striding across the lawn.

"My God, we all thought you were dead. The firemen said they might never find a body in there, if there was one."

Tucker turned back to where he house was supposed to be. It still wasn't there. "No. I wasn't home."

"Well, thank God for that. Where were you?"

"Fishing. In Minnesota."

"Man, you should have seen it last night. Must have been six or seven trucks here. I had to get out and turn the hose on my roof so it wouldn't spread."

"What happened?"

"Don't know. We heard a bang like some kind of explosion and by the time I looked out my window the whole thing was in flames. Must have been a gas leak. That's what we all figured last night. I don't know what else it could be."

"Yeah. Gas leak. Probably."

Bill put a hand on Tucker's shoulder, the first time the two men had ever touched in nine years of being neighbors. "You gonna be all right, buddy?"

Tucker looked deep into the black heart of the wreckage. He felt like he was staring into his own scorched heart.

"I'll be okay. I can stay at my dad's place."

"Hey, you need anything. You give me a call." Bill patted Tucker's shoulder like a dad sending his kid up to bat in a little league game.

"Thanks, Bill."

"No problem. We're just glad you're alive. Last night we all... well, we about held you a funeral."

"Yeah."

He drove back to Webb's place slow and steady, more passenger than driver. As soon as he stepped inside he said, "Call Stanley again. Tell him we make this deal now or we walk away."

Calvin turned off the TV. "Fine. You okay?"

"No. Not really."

"Look, Tucker, I'm sorry about Jenny. Maybe I shouldn't have done it, but she's the one who took the money and run off."

"Yeah. You were right. Is that what you want to hear?"

185

"No. I want to make sure your anger is aimed in the right direction. Anger aimed in the wrong place can get mighty ugly."

"What the hell do you think the last two weeks has been?" Calvin braced himself. He could tell the flood was coming. "I've been aiming it at the Stanleys over Dad. I've been aiming it at Jenny for three years now over my mistakes in our marriage. I've been aiming it at you since you came here, but I can't say you didn't deserve at least most of it."

"You call that anger? Hell, Tuck, why didn't you pop me one if you felt like it? Why didn't you jump across Hugh's desk and knock out his teeth with an ashtray? Keeping it all inside will kill you."

"I was following you. You agreed to work for them. You took me on those jobs and you made it clear you were in charge."

"Hell, Tucker, If I waited for you we'd still be sitting waiting for the Stanleys to come take ten million in cash or flesh. And up until our little trip here, we didn't have it in cash."

"Fine. So now I'm showing my anger. I'm letting it all hang out. Call Stanley. Find out who the fuck killed my dad and bring him to me. I'll show you what anger looks like when it's aimed in the right direction."

Calvin sat still feeling a heat come off Tucker he'd never felt before.

"Okay then."

Tucker tried to loosen his jaw. His eyes ran down the hall. "What about Milo. Did you tell him yet?"

"I told him."

"What did you say?"

"I kept it simple. Figured you should be the one to fill in

the details."

"Thanks." Tucker took two steps toward the back bedroom then stopped, his back to Calvin. "They burned down my house."

"They what?"

"Last night. They burned it down. Everything's gone. Everything."

Calvin's fist tightened. "We're not staying in this crap town anymore anyhow."

"Yeah."

"Burn the whole thing down for all I care."

Tucker walked down the hall and Calvin stepped into the kitchen to make the call.

Calvin recognized the voice of the blonde receptionist. "Put him on the phone. He knows who the fuck it is." There was a click and some smooth jazz played. After thirty seconds Hugh picked up.

"Cal, that you?"

"Nice try on the match job. Missed your mark though."

"Oh yeah? We weren't sure. The boys didn't stick around to find out."

"You gonna blame that on Kirby too?"

"No, no. You boys have become my problem too now. So what is it you're looking for? I assume you still want to make some sort of deal?"

"Same as it was. I want who killed Webb served to me on a silver platter and you get your money."

Calvin could hear Hugh's jaw working on grinding his teeth down further.

"Even swap?"

"Even Steven."

"You know I can't give you Kirby."

"I know he hasn't pulled a trigger or fired up a chainsaw for any head cutting in years. I'll take what you give me. And you take what I give you, even if it's a little light."

"You spent some of my money?"

"Call it fire insurance."

More teeth grinding. Hugh was going to need a dentist by the end of this conversation.

"Cal, we've known each other a long time."

"A long time."

"If this is really the walkaway, let's do it no bullshit. No funny business. I need that money and I'm tired of slugging it out with you boys. If this was thirty years ago you know your ass would already be separated from your head and sitting next to your son in our little secret spot."

"That spot ought to be designated a historical landmark, all the bodies you got in there."

"I'm going to make this deal out of respect for what our families have meant to each other over the years. But, after this, if I ever see you again, your name won't mean shit."

"Hugh, after this if you ever see me again it will mean we're both dead and the devil made us roommates."

"Fine."

"You say where and when."

***

Tucker sat on the bed next to his son, both staring forward at the carpet.

Milo said he understood, but how could he? Maybe he'd

seen the side of Jenny Tucker had always been blind to. Something made him want to get away from her. He'd gotten his wish.

"So I think we'll be moving soon. I'm not sure where yet. I'll have to see where I can open another insurance office. Shouldn't be too hard. That is if I haven't pissed off too many clients here yet. With the internet a bad rating can dog you for a long time."

"I'm sure we'll be fine, Dad."

"Well, then you're one up on me."

Milo let his dad have his moment. He knew he should have told him about the note, but he didn't. Jenny asked him specifically not to in her goodbye letter. She didn't bother to explain. She wrote that as hard as it was, she thought it would be what Milo wanted. He'd been trying so hard to get away from her recently that having her out of the picture might make him happier. In case he ever needed her she left a cell phone number. Strictly confidential. *Don't tell your dad.*

Milo read the single page ten times in a row. The ending never changed. *Goodbye. Mom.*

27

Milo helped them load the eleven remaining boxes into the truck even though he had no idea where his dad and granddad were going.

"Thanks," Tucker said.

"Be safe, okay?" Milo knew what it meant if he wasn't on the need-to-know clearance level about their latest meeting. "Don't get killed. You're kinda all I have right now."

"You don't have to say it like it's a bad thing."

"It's only bad if you don't come home."

Tucker hugged his son, patted him twice firmly on the back and climbed into the cab of the truck.

Tucker and Calvin drove in silence. It could have been the street lights, but Tucker felt Calvin looked old. He knew that Calvin was old but since he showed up from Omaha he had aged quite a bit. Might have been the lack of beer intake. Calvin had been a teetotaler all day.

It was close to midnight and neither one of them had gotten decent night's sleep in several days. For a man in his late 80s he looked okay, but he looked his age.

The meeting place was deep into a wooded area near a lake where Tucker used to come fishing with his dad and Calvin when he was a boy. Rain began to fall but not in any way you'd call committed, more like the sky had started to sweat.

They passed the cutoff that took you down to the water and continued up toward the crest of a small hill. As they started to climb they passed three black Hummers all parked at the bottom. Tucker and Calvin exchanged a look.

"Is it me," Calvin said. "Or is this what an ambush looks like?"

"If it's an ambush they sure are lousy at hiding."

The road angled sharply to the left and Tucker slowed the truck to make the turn. Branches scraped along the top of the truck's payload sounding like a Halloween sound effects record. The tires spun momentarily on the sweat-soaked ground at the start of an incline and Tucker dropped the gear into Low and eased down onto the gas until the truck gripped and started climbing slowly.

They reached the top of the hill and were greeted by six men all standing in a semicircle around a figure in a chair. Each of the six men held a road flare in one hand lighting the night sky in a red misty glow.

The row of beefy men looked like the offensive line from the '86 Bears, but wearing matching black suits with no ties. The man on the outer edge of the semicircle held up a hand motioning Tucker to stop.

He parked the truck a good thirty yards from the chair.

"Well," Calvin said reaching into the glove box and taking out a revolver. "Here goes nothing."

The air outside clung damp to the trees slick with the thin rain and the hissing sound of the flares sounded like a forest full of cicadas whispering. The moon and stars were blocked by high clouds so the flares were the only light. It gave Tucker the impression of being at the bottom of a giant well.

As they approached the men they could see more clearly the figure strapped down. He sat in a folding lawn chair, duct tape bound his arms to the chair and his legs to the thin metal of the base. More tape covered his mouth and looped around his head several times. He sucked air in and out through his nose but Tucker saw dried blood crusted around each nostril. A matching pair of shiners adorned each eye.

The same man who raised his hand spoke. "Here's your man."

"This the one that killed Webb?" Calvin asked.

"This is the man we were told to bring to you."

Calvin nodded, eyeing the trapped man up and down.

The Stanley man swiveled his flare to point at the ground as he checked his watch. "You have something for us?"

Tucker gestured over his shoulder to the truck while holding out the keys in front of him. "How do we get home?"

"We'll leave one of the Hummers." The man held out a set of keys of his own.

He and Tucker engaged in a short game of chicken, each one daring the other silently to throw their keys first. Calvin kept staring at the man lashed to the chair.

Finally the man brought his arm back and launched the Hummer keys forward. Tucker did the same and the sets of keys passed by in the moist air. Tucker's throw was wild so the man next to his target had to lean to snatch them out of the air, but the Hummer keys came straight into Tucker's palm.

The six men all began walking in formation. Tucker and Calvin both tensed. The men passed by them with no regard for the man in the chair. Tucker and Calvin each had a flare placed in their hands without a word.

The men who had been talking looked at his watch again. "Let's move out." The men all began to walk double-time like a military exercise.

Four men trotted down the hill while two got in the truck and started it. The rain morphed from a mist to droplets, gaining confidence.

Tucker turned to the man in the chair.

Like anyone duct taped to a chair and beaten, he pleaded for his life. His head moved violently around, his eyes wild with things to say, a case to plead. The hissing of the flares roared in Tucker's ears like standing too close to a blast furnace.

Calvin gripped the revolver, tightening and loosening his fingers around the gun.

The man bucked and rocked the chair, trying to get away or make his case by charades.

Calvin abruptly handed the gun to Tucker.

"Here. You do it."

Tucker regarded the revolver like Calvin had just shoved a pile of shit in his hand.

"Why me?"

"I thought you wanted to."

"Well..."

He looked at the man's eyes. That was a mistake. He understood why executioners used a black hood.

"I don't want to."

Behind them they heard the truck downshift into low and then a crunch. The mud they encountered on the way up had apparently got the best of the truck on the way down. Next came the grinding of reverse gears.

"What do you mean you don't want to?"

Tucker turned away from the man. "Look, why don't we admit that we're not this kind of guy. We're drivers. We don't kill people in cold blood."

"He killed your dad."

"So okay, he did. I'm sure it wasn't his idea." The man's wild eyes rattled in his head as he nodded the affirmative. "If we do this we're no better. And we are better."

Calvin's face was carved deep with shadowed lines from the flare. His eyebrows bent with the struggle his mind worked over. For a moment he was that confused old man lost at the mall.

Tucker stared at his granddad. "We're not them. We're McGraws."

Calvin sniffed back tears. "You're right."

Down the hill they heard gears grind again.

Calvin tossed down his flare and dug in his back pocket for his knife. He unfolded a blade about the size of a lady's pinky finger and went at the man in the chair.

At first the man's eyes went wide again, but when Calvin started sawing at the tape around his mouth he began to weep. His face already glistened with sweat in the glow of the flares and now snot mixed with the dried blood and made it smear again over the silver tape.

It took Calvin a few hacking motions to cut through the four layers of duct tape, but he got a loose end and pulled it around the man's head, pulling tufts of hair as it went.

When the man's mouth was free he coughed as he tried to speak. A fine spray of blood came from his mouth in the same tiny red sparks as the flares.

"Unhook me!"

His panic seemed undiminished even knowing his killers had turned his saviors.

"Relax pal, we're not gonna kill you," Calvin said as he stepped around to a leg of the chair to start sawing.

"You gotta get this vest off me. We're all gonna die."

Tucker brought his flare around to see the man's eyes more clearly.

"What do you mean?"

"C4. They strapped me with it. To kill us all."

Calvin reached up and tore open the man's plaid shirt. He wore a kevlar vest taped with four small rectangles each with wires leading out. He turned over his shoulder and looked at Tucker.

"Cut him loose."

The man bucked the chair more in a frenzy.

"Sit still," commanded Calvin as he started in on the tape with his impotent blade.

Tucker stepped forward. "Is it on a timer or is someone going to trigger it?"

"Timer."

Tucker remembered the Stanley man checking his watch and telling his men to hurry up.

"Bring that light over here," Calvin said. Tucker swung the flare down low so Calvin could see what he was cutting.

Tucker looked back at the man. "Did you kill my father?"

"I don't know who it was. I just followed orders."

"From who? From Kirby?"

"How the hell could Kirby give any orders? For fuck's sake, cut faster."

A tiny crack could barely be heard over the steady white noise of the flare. Calvin's sawing motions stopped. Tucker looked down. The knife blade had snapped.

Calvin's eyes met his. They asked, do we run?

"Keep trying."

Tucker dropped his flare and began clawing at the tape around the man's wrists. The tape was layered and thick and wet with rain. He continued his questioning with a deep seated feeling that this might be his only chance.

"Why can't Kirby give any orders?"

"He's an invalid. A half-wit. Ever since the accident. Can't even wipe his own ass."

Hugh lied. Tucker tried to meet Calvin's eyes but his granddad was too busy pulling at the tape, his fingers sliding off each time he tried to search for the start of the tape with his fingernail.

"What happened?"

"Hunting accident. Blew half his face off with his own gun. Will you hurry the fuck up."

A tearing sound came from down low. Calvin pulled a loose end of the tape off the right leg of the chair. He unwound the spool eight times around until the leg came loose.

Tucker found the end of the tape on his right hand. He pulled and the sound of duct tape tearing brought a crazed laugh to the man in the chair.

Another eight loops around were made difficult by the man's moving and tugging at his arm trying to break free even a millisecond sooner.

When Tucker pulled the last bit of tape free the man immediately clamped his right hand down on his left and started tearing at the tape. He stood with his one free leg and spun the chair knocking Calvin away into the soaked ground. His jeans immediately took on water.

"Get the vest off," Calvin said. "Don't worry about the legs."

The wild man ignored him. The laugh turned to more coughing as the trapped man spun like a wild dervish in the wet grass on the ridge top. Calvin rolled out of the way and almost spun himself on top of a flare.

The man started moving faster, running away before he was free.

"Wait," Tucker said.

Calvin put a hand on the ground and pushed himself up. He snatched the flare as he stood and put his free hand in the crook of Tucker's elbow.

"We gotta go."

Calvin pulled Tucker along backwards as he watched the man in the chair hopping and stumbling toward the trees clawing at his wrist and shaking the vest trying to release it from his chest.

Calvin tripped forward keeping one foot barely beneath him as he pulled Tucker down the incline back the way they drove in. In his retreat he could see the taillights of the truck and two Hummers making their way down the trail. The truck had finally gotten free, but the men had been too preoccupied to hear it.

Tucker turned his body and joined Calvin in retreat. They'd gotten three steps in unison when the blast came.

Both men were thrown to the ground. The explosion echoed from the top of the hill. Tucker wasn't sure how much time had passed before he found himself sitting up. The flares had gone out. He turned to Calvin who was rubbing his head.

The sound of debris falling through the trees told Tucker he wasn't out of it for long. He patted his pocket and felt what he wanted—keys.

"Come on." Tucker tugged at Calvin's sleeve as he stood up.

"What are we gonna do?"

"What we do best. We're gonna drive."

28

Tucker behind the wheel of the Hummer, pounding through the woods on some sort of internal navigation, gave Calvin a sweet déjà vu. Memories of his own forest runs came flooding back with each buck and pitch of the vehicle. Those sweet days when a few cases of booze were all that was at stake. When the gun in his glove box went ten years without being fired. Simpler times.

Calvin barked direction even though there was only one road leading away from the lake. Stating the obvious made him feel useful.

The windshield wipers slammed back and forth as the rain fell in earnest now.

"Are we stupid? Is that it?" Tucker asked.

"No, we ain't stupid. We don't think like they do. That ain't a bad thing."

"I don't want to be like them."

"We're not."

Tucker had to shout over the engine and the rain. "I don't want to be a criminal."

"You're not a criminal, kid."

"Goddammit, Granddad. Can't you see what we've done? It's time I owned up to it. I'm a McGraw, through and through."

"I'll give you that." The Hummer dipped into a rut on the dirt road. Both men came up out of their seats for a second before crashing down again. Tucker kept the wheels straight and true. "But, McGraw men are not criminals." Calvin turned to Tucker who flicked his eyes off the road for a moment to meet him. "We're outlaws."

Tucker turned onto more solid road. He stabbed his foot down on the accelerator.

"I can live with that."

Up ahead tiny red dots wavered in the air like fireflies. Tucker bore down on them. The back of the line was another Hummer, then the cube truck, then a Hummer out front.

"What do I do?" Tucker asked.

"Spin him."

"How?"

"Put your right headlight on his left taillight and cut the wheel. He'll fishtail out and you hit the brakes. Don't ram him. We need this car for the rest of it."

Tucker tightened his grip on the wheel. The engine revved angry as he angled the front corner of his black behemoth into the back end of its twin.

"Now cut it right," Calvin said.

Tucker turned the wheel.

"Brake."

Both men were pulled taut into their seat belts as the Hummer slowed. The black car in front of them veered wildly then overcorrected and swung across both lanes of the wet asphalt.

"Amateur," Calvin scolded.

The Hummer ahead of them dove off into the ditch like a dog after a squirrel. The front end hit the upside of the ditch and came up like a shark breeching the water and rolled until the three-ton vehicle came down on the hood in a field of seedling soybeans.

Tucker sped up again, feeling a surge of adrenalin as he hunted down the next in line.

Calvin smiled a prideful grin. "Go get 'em."

The Hummer in front slowed and so did the cube truck behind it. The loss of a colleague seemed to come as a surprise. Tucker pulled his Hummer alongside the cube truck, Calvin's door facing the driver of the truck.

Calvin could see the man's confused and angry face and recognized him as the one who did all the talking.

A shot rang out from a big gun. Tucker saw a man leaning out of the passenger door of the Hummer ahead. He fired again and a bullet ripped into the hood with a dull metallic clank.

"You still have your gun?" Tucker asked.

"Yeah, but it's not gonna do us any good. We gotta bait 'em. Head for the ditch."

"What?"

"The ditch. Trust me. Don't hit it too fast."

Another shot blasted the night like the rainstorm decided it needed some thunder but couldn't make its own.

"Now!"

Tucker hit the brakes and veered to his left and aimed the Hummer down into the ditch. The car dipped and lost traction for a moment before hitting the far end of the ditch and grinding to a stop.

"Get out." Calvin was already undoing his buckle. "We did this once in '55 with a gang of feds. Worked like a charm."

Tucker stepped down out of the car and his foot sank above his ankles in water and mud. He pulled hard to get his leg out and followed Calvin around the back of car and across the road to the ditch on the other side.

Down the road the twin sets of taillights glowed side by side as if a conference was going on between drivers. The Hummer turned first and the cube truck followed. They came cautiously through the rain to where the discarded Hummer leaned on its side, engine still running and lights still on save for the broken left headlamp.

Both vehicles aimed their lights at the broken Hummer in the ditch and idled.

Determined not to let their prey escape again the Hummer emptied of its men, both carrying the same large caliber guns. The cube truck opened its doors and two men got out. The one who had spoken earlier called out commands.

"You two take the far side. Watch your crossfire."

The four men fanned out taking a military style approach to the crippled vehicle. They ignored the rain as if they didn't have time to be bothered. Each held a frightening looking gun out ahead of them in a two-handed grip.

They rounded the Hummer from all sides, moving slow and checking the field beyond for movement.

Crouched in the ditch on the opposite side of the road, Calvin tapped Tucker's shoulder. He moved first in a fast but quiet crouch-walk practiced over decades of hunting animals even more skittish than the gunmen circling across the road.

Tucker followed, trying to match his granddad's footsteps exactly. He hated being wet and by then he was soaked to the bone, but he felt grateful for the rain since the sound masked what little noise they made.

Calvin reached the cube truck first and slid in through the driver's side. Tucker followed. Calvin stayed low and Tucker did the same.

"Hate to say it, Tuck, but you're gonna have to pop up so you can see over the dash while you drive."

Tucker knew it. He also knew he didn't have much time.

"Do your family name proud, son," Calvin said.

Tucker flattened his foot down on the pedal as he swung himself up to see barely over the dash and turned the wheel hard to the left. He let the momentum of the turn slam the door shut for him as he aimed the truck down the road back in the direction they came, not confident enough to attempt a U-turn with four armed men blocking his path.

Bullets pelted the payload of the truck and if they didn't know better they would have sworn it started to hail.

"Come on truck," Tucker said. "Go faster Goddamn you."

Calvin whooped with laughter and slapped his hands down on the dashboard in an impromptu drum solo.

"Worked exactly like it did in '55."

"Yeah? You got away?"

"Well, I'm here ain't I?"

"You said you went to prison once."

"That wasn't it."

Tucker checked his side view mirror and saw headlights.

"Did this happen in '55?"

Calvin checked his mirror. "Shit. It sure did."

"What?" Tucker veered into the oncoming lane. He corrected his course and continued to floor it. "What did you do?"

"We started throwing bottles of moonshine at them. Crashed 'em up good."

"We don't have any bottles."

Tucker began calculating where he was and how long it would be before another turn off, hopefully into a populated area where they could possibly lose the tail. Nothing came to mind. They were thirty miles from nowhere, and in Iowa that was saying something.

"Let's see what we got." Calvin spun himself around on his seat and reached up behind the bench to a small access panel between the cab of the truck and the payload. The opening was no bigger than an air duct, but big enough for an 86-year-old man with no plan B.

"What are you doing?"

"Trying something."

Calvin hoisted himself up and through the panel, landing with a thud.

"You okay?" Tucker called over his shoulder.

"Yep. Gonna hurt tomorrow," Calvin called back.

If we make it to tomorrow, Tucker thought.

Calvin felt around his waist. No gun.

"Tucker."

"What?"

"I dropped my gun."

Tucker spun his head around the cab of the truck. At first he didn't see anything, but he spotted the pistol on the floor near the far door where Calvin had been sitting.

"I guess you need it, huh?"

"I could try throwing insults at them, but that hasn't worked so far."

Tucker rolled his eyes and shook his head even though no

one was looking to see it. He leaned as far as he could while keeping one hand on the wheel and he was still a good two feet away. The road ahead ran straight so Tucker inhaled deeply, made sure the wheel was centered and let go. He lunged to his side, lifting his foot off the gas, and swooped up the gun with his right hand. He sat up quickly, almost giving himself a head rush, and grabbed the wheel again with his left. He put his foot back down on the accelerator, angry that he had to lift off at all and give them even a bit of a chance to catch up.

He pushed the gun through the panel over his shoulder and heard the pistol land on the metal floor of the payload.

"Thanks," came through with a hollow sound like Calvin was speaking to him through a tin can tied to a string.

Inside the cube was loud from the thin metal walls being battered by the rain, a simple spring storm turned into a tempest by Tucker's lead foot pushing them past 80 down the straight stretch of country highway.

Calvin saw four neat round holes in the back roll door from the volley of bullets that fired as they sped away. He grabbed the walls for stability as he walked back to the door. Tucker's driving was steady and felt more like riding in the boxcar of a train than in a high-speed chase. Calvin stepped up and put his eye to one of the holes and saw the bright xenon headlights of the Hummer approaching.

He turned and took stock of the truck. Eleven banker's boxes filled with money. Two thick quilted movers blankets. The empty cardboard spindle from a roll of packing tape.

That was it.

The first shot rang out from the Hummer. Nothing pierced the truck so they couldn't have been too close, but close enough that someone felt like taking a shot.

Calvin thought back to '55. He wasn't misremembering, was he? They did get away from the feds?

Yep. He could still see and smell the moonshine as each bottle smashed on the windshield of the G-men's Ford.

If it worked once...

Calvin tore through the packing tape and opened a banker's box. He took out a stack of hundred-dollar bills. The paper band around the money said $10,000. One hundred rectangles of paper. It was no moonshine, but the distraction might make them think enough for him to get off a shot.

Calvin rolled the door up a foot. Spray from the road and the back tires spat over his shoes. The Hummer was close enough now he could hear the engine.

He crouched to his knees and looked. Twenty feet away the grille of the black car looked angry, furious for being made a fool of. Calvin tore off the paper band binding the stack of bills together and sidearmed a throw through the opening.

Once out in the 80-mile-an-hour backdraft of the truck the bills took flight and spread like confetti fired from a canon. Most of the bills scattered to the pavement but some ended up on the hood of the car and some made it on to the windshield, sticking to the rain.

Calvin felt he was on to something. The wiper blades shoved most of the bills away but they were stubborn, thin enough to slide under the rubber of the wipers.

Calvin undid another bundle and held it outside, letting the bills soak up some water before he threw. With more direct aim he hurled the next batch at the window. Again they scattered and again several clung to the windshield.

For his effort he got a flurry of gunfire back.

Bullets pierced the metal sides of the cube, passing through like they were balsa wood. Calvin didn't know where to duck for cover so he stood still, hand on another stack of bills in the open box next to him. When the burst of gunfire was over he repeated his soak and throw action. A few bills from the last throw still clung to the glass, the paper starting to tear under the constant passing of the wiper blades.

He sent another hundred bills out into the night and got another six bullets back, two of them tearing through the roll door dangerously close to him.

As he turned to lift another stack from the box he noticed, as if for the first time, the two movers blankets. In his mind they had Ben Franklin printed all over them.

Tucker waged an internal debate. Keep on the straightaway or weave to avoid the gun blasts? If he started swerving like mad Calvin would topple over and whatever he was doing back there would be impossible. But what was he doing back there?

"You okay?"

"Doing fine. Keep her steady."

That answered his question.

Calvin balled up the movers blanket in one hand. It was heavy and the quilting was frayed in spots. He patted the gun in his belt, resting on his hip like an old west sheriff ready for the draw.

He bent down and lifted fast on the roll door. He let go when the door was on its way and let inertia take the steel the rest of the way up so he could get a two-handed grip on the blanket and heave.

The Hummer had come close, angling for a pass, so Calvin

had to adjust his throw at the last second to aim more to the right. The blanket unfurled as it flew and moved like a giant bat in the night, whipping and changing shape as it sailed.

The single flat wing landed on the hood and spread out across the windshield where it stuck. Calvin could see a tiny triangle of glass on the driver's side but the space was hardly enough to drive by.

The Hummer swerved.

Calvin drew.

"You brung this on yourself, you little shits."

He fired his .38 in a pale imitation of the roaring large caliber blasts that had been lobbed at him all night. Three shots, all grouped around the same front tire. He heard a pop and a hiss and the Hummer ducked like it was a football player taking a knee, only at eighty miles an hour.

Sparks flew from the front end and the car spun around the point where the frame dug into the road. The asphalt proved unforgiving and held the corner of the Hummer to a stop while the rest of the car went past, flipping it up and over the nose to land hard on the roof.

Calvin slid down onto the bench seat head first through the panel, bumping Tucker as he did.

"What happened?"

"Take us home. We've got planning to do."

29

Calvin fed another quarter into the payphone. Tucker's cell phone was dead and it took them a half hour of driving around to find one before they spotted the silver box on a pole in the far end of the diner's parking lot.

"Tell me again why you had to make this call now?" Tucker asked. "You said go home."

"I know I did but I gotta see it for myself first. It'll effect the plans we make."

Someone on the other end of the line picked up.

"Georgia darlin'? It's Cal McGraw."

"Cal who?" The old woman was still half asleep. More than half.

"Calvin McGraw. Sorry to call you so late, Georgia."

"Cal McGraw, what in the hell?"

"I need to ask you a question and I wouldn't do it if I wasn't in a spot of trouble. I need to know what happened to Kirby Stanley."

"Kirby? Why you need to know that for?"

"Can you just tell me if he's alright."

"He's alright if you don't forget to change his feeding bag."

Calvin turned to Tucker and raised his eyebrows. "Is that right, darlin'?"

"Got shot in the head. Right through his left eye. Can't speak, can't walk. They call him a, what do you call it... a vegetable."

"Where's he at, Georgia?"

"Why do you want to know all this, Cal?"

"I told you I'm in a mess of trouble with Hugh. Things sure ain't what they used to be."

"You can say that again. Used to be a man wouldn't call someone in the middle of the goddamn night. Especially a lady. Especially a lady he hasn't talked to in ten years." She thought about it. "More like twenty."

"Tell me where I can find Kirby and I'll leave you be."

"He's in a hospice over in Coralville. Nurses twenty-four hours a day. Him and all the invalids live over there. Called whispering pines or weeping willow or some damn thing. I don't know, it's too late."

"That's good enough darlin'. I thank you, Georgia. You always were the one that got away."

"I only got away 'cause I ran so damn fast whenever you came around, Cal. I get the feeling I should still be running."

"Thanks, Peach. Be seeing you."

"Not if I see you first."

The line went dead. Calvin turned to Tucker.

"Point that thing for Coralville."

Another payphone outside a public library in Coralville turned up that rarest of things—a phone book. Waterlogged and bloated it still had a legible section on nursing homes and hospice care that listed a Willow Creek less than half a mile from where they parked.

The night nurse wore slippers as she answered the door.

"Don't knock so damn loud or you'll wake the patients. Now who the hell are you two?"

Tucker hung back behind Calvin who spoke. "We need to see Kirby Stanley."

The nurse, fitting firmly into the category of sassy black woman, thrust out a hip in defiance.

"I don't know if you can tell, but it ain't exactly visiting hours right now. You all can come back later."

"It'll take all of five minutes."

Tucker put a hand on Calvin's arm. "He's here, that's all we need to know."

"No, I need to see him."

"You best listen to your friend here. Don't make me call the po-lice on your ass."

"I won't wake anybody up unless you make me."

Calvin pushed forward placing an arm across the nurse's chest and forcing her open like a swinging door. Tucker followed to make sure Calvin didn't do anything stupid.

"Hey!" Sassy black nurse realized her own volume and hushed her voice. "Hey. You can't be in here."

Calvin found a room chart on the wall. The alphabetically arranged chart made it easy to find Stanley—38.

Tucker tried to placate the angry nurse. "We'll only be a second."

Calvin moved quickly forward down the hall.

The nurse moved quickly behind him, her slippers sliding silently across the tile floor.

Tucker moved in her footsteps right behind her. "We're not going to do anything but look. We really will be out in five minutes."

She crooked a single eyebrow up as she looked over her shoulder at Tucker. He smiled at her.

Calvin reached door 38 and turned the knob and pushed the door open slowly. He stood in the doorway, the nurse and Tucker stopped behind him. The three of them sat still in the hall like tombstones.

Inside the room Calvin saw a figure of such menace and fear in earlier days reduced to a science fiction comic book of beeping machines, green LED lights, the steady wheeze of artificial breathing and the stale smell of cleansers and a urine bag waiting until morning to be emptied.

Kirby Stanley. Even the name would strike fear into men enough to make them leave the state. If they could see him now. A breathing tube hung from a tracheotomy hole, drool dried in white lines like old snail trails ran down from the corners of his mouth. In the light from the open window shade Calvin could see the missing eye and a deep indent above where the bones in Kirby's skull had to be removed.

He wanted to run around the room and pull all the plugs, not to end Kirby's suffering, but to end his own. Seeing a human life sustained by tricks and fakery hurt Calvin's heart. He wanted to tell Tucker not to let him get that far gone. Smother him with a pillow if need be.

Calvin turned. "Thank you for your time, ma'am."

He passed by quietly. Tucker followed. "Thank you."

The nurse stood still, tightening her cardigan around her.

They arrived back at Webb's at 3:30 in the morning. Tucker turned off the truck, but they both sat in the cab as the engine knocked.

"So it was Hugh," Tucker said.

"Seems that way."

"He lied to our faces."

"Yep."

"He killed Webb."

"Did that too."

Webb's house, previously only used for beer drinking and watching Burt Reynolds movies, had been turned in a headquarters for a new venture tentatively titled Revenge Inc. The title only lived in Calvin's head.

"What happened out there?" Milo asked as he brought two cold cans of PBR for his dad and granddad.

Calvin cracked the seal on his and inhaled the foam off the top. "They tried to fuck us is what. I know a boy at your age would entertain the idea of a fucking from about anywhere and anyone but trust me, this is not the kind of fucking you'd want."

Tucker was beyond scolding Calvin for his language. "So what's the plan?" he asked.

"We bring it right to him. We go see Hugh."

"Okay. Then what?"

"I'm not so sure. I'm not even sure we can get in the door."

Tucker set down his beer, unopened. "How do we hurt him? Y'know, without actually hurting him. I'm still not ready to become a killer. Any more than we've had to." He turned to his son. "And we had to, otherwise we'd be dead."

Milo nodded with understanding.

"It's the truth," Calvin said before pulling deep on the can of beer.

"The money," Tucker said. "He needs it or he's going to go

under, right?"

"It sure sounds that way."

"Well, I sure as hell don't want it anymore."

"What are you saying?"

Tucker stared into an empty bowl meant to hold fruit, but that held only dust. "I'm saying I think I know how to hurt him."

"What about the money though?"

"We can't keep it."

"Says who?"

"It's blood money. It's tainted. It's got bad luck all over it."

"I'll ask again, says who?"

Tucker leveled a stare at Calvin. "Says me."

Calvin stared right back. "If you go by that logic then every dollar your dad used to raise you was blood money and bad luck. I never heard you complain before. And you haven't exactly been running a lucky streak."

"I'm not winning the lottery."

Calvin continued to meet Tucker's eyes. "Your numbers just hit big, Tuck. Those boxes are the payoff."

"I don't want it. I'm not a criminal." Calvin opened his mouth to lay into his grandson. Tucker raised a hand to cut him off. "After tonight."

Milo sat on the arm of the couch watching the two older men square off. He watched Calvin's shoulders sink a little, the fight going out of him.

"It's a damn stupid thing."

"I'm not going to have my son raised on that money. No matter how easy it would make things. I'm going to show him that being a McGraw means being an honest man. A man who defends his family when they've been wronged, but a man

214

who will not steal and will not make excuses for what can be gained by other people stealing."

Calvin sat quietly, a fingernail tapping on the half-empty can.

"Can you get me into Hugh Stanley's house?" Tucker asked.

"I think I can. I need the boy though." Calvin turned to Milo. "You ready for your first job?"

"Yes, sir. Ready as I'll ever be."

30

"I never thought in a million fucking years a giant refrigerator on wheels would be my primary mode of transportation." Calvin sulked in the passenger seat with Milo sandwiched between him and Tucker.

The white truck wound through residential streets in an area of hundred-plus year-old houses with wide lawns. Calvin gave directions to Tucker who steered the truck to the curb in front of Hugh Stanley's house, a three-level with a wraparound porch and two imposing oak trees in the yard.

Nothing about the house distinguished it as a drug kingpin's home or set it apart from his university professor neighbors.

Tucker compared the house to the Scarface image he held in his mind. There was no gaudy opulence or row of Italian cars. No Roman columns or teams of roaming bodyguards or electrics fences. There was no fence at all. This was Iowa after all.

Tucker figured a life of crime would buy you more than a nice home in a suburban college town. He remembered what his dad had always said about the Stanleys being big fish in a small pond. Now he knew what that meant, and this pond had a little scum on the surface, a few too many dead leaves sunk to the bottom.

The three generations of men stepped down out of the truck and made their way along the driveway to a two-car garage. They passed a little two-door Japanese sports car with after market add-ons like a rear spoiler and flared bumpers that made the whole thing look ridiculous. Easy to rule the two-door out as Hugh's car, but it would become integral to the plan.

When they reached the garage a few yards later Tucker pulled at the handle and the door began to slide up. He paused and moved it as slow as he could to remain quiet.

Calvin searched for surveillance cameras but found none. He watched the door for signs of movement, but all remained quiet.

Once the garage door was lifted all the way, Calvin took over.

They snuck in and stood next to a four-door Mercedes in black. Calvin had never gone for German cars. Too stiff. Good engines, but if you ended up with a bad back the rest of your life it wasn't worth it.

He produced a slim jim from his coat and guided Milo in the art of breaking into a car. Tucker tried not to watch. What had he let his son play party to?

Calvin slid the strip of metal between the window and door frame then handed it to Milo.

"You gotta work it around a little bit, but you'll feel it catch. Just like hooking a bass. When you feel it hit, you jerk it up and get it to set."

Milo stared off at nothing while he felt the slender metal tool tapping against the inner workings of the car door. Tucker began to bounce on his heels, impatient. Calvin turned to him and silently put a finger to his lips to shush and calm Tucker down so as not to unnerve the boy.

Milo kept at it for a good three minutes. "I can't feel it."

"Son, you ever been with a woman?"

Milo was speechless. Tucker broke in. "What the hell does that have to do with it?"

"Answer me yes or no, you ever been with a woman?"

"What do you mean been with?"

"Oh, for Christ sake." Tucker stepped out of the garage to scope out the front of the house.

Calvin turned to Milo once Tucker had left. "He's gone, you can tell me."

"Not, like, sex but..."

"You've felt around a pussy at least?"

"A little bit." Even in the dim light of the garage Milo's blushing was obvious.

"Then you know what a delicate touch it takes. This is the same thing." Calvin put a hand over Milo's on the slim jim and guided them both together. "You move it around. That slot in the slim jim is waiting to meet the perfect match. They're meant to go together like a man and a woman. You ease it around, don't go jamming it in and poking at everything you feel. Just like a woman, you go slow. She'll thank you for it. So will the car."

Calvin pulled up sharply on the slim jim and the door lock sprang up. He smiled, remembering days of women and cars and how he could make either one do whatever he wanted. Those were good days.

Milo grinned at his first B&E.

As Calvin ran Milo through the fine art of hot-wiring a

car, Tucker crept slowly to the window on the first floor of the house. The curtains were drawn and he could see nothing but the soft yellow light from inside. He checked his watch: 5:25 A.M.

Behind him, the Mercedes came to life. He turned and could see a fine mist of exhaust steam rising out of the garage door in the early morning chill. He moved back to his son and granddad.

Milo sat behind the wheel proudly, his hands gripping the leather-wrapped steering wheel. Calvin patted the boy on the shoulder and stood straight.

"You ready?" he asked Tucker.

"I guess so."

"I can't change your mind?"

"I thought you agreed."

Calvin shook his head once, not believing he'd ever agreed to giving away that money. "I guess I did. Worth a shot though. It's a lot of money."

"That money killed my father."

"No, whatever was in that semi-truck killed Webb. You're taking it out on a bunch of innocent Ben Franklins."

"I'll go in alone if you want."

"No, no. We go together. This is family business."

They walked to the door as Milo eased the Mercedes out of the garage and left it idling in the driveway in clear view.

Tucker knocked. They both stood and began to feel the cold for the first time as they waited for someone to answer. Calvin stepped forward and pounded on the door with a balled up fist before returning his hands to a fold behind his back.

The door opened and young man in a dark suit stood there looking pissed off. The night security. The owner of the

Japanese car. Also the owner of a gun he held down by his thigh in his right hand.

Calvin spoke first, implementing his plan that he claimed had worked sometime in the mid-fifties.

"Don't look now but someone is stealing your car."

He and Tucker both moved aside and Milo saw his cue to rev the engine a few times.

The gunman looked at his boss' car then at the two men on the porch. He had obviously been woken from sleeping on the job and the situation was coming to him a little slowly. Calvin helped his understanding along.

"Better get moving if you want to catch him." Behind his back he waved one hand and Milo saw his second cue. The car dropped into gear and began racing backward down the driveway.

The gunman blinked twice and then bolted out of the house after the car. As he passed, Tucker loosed the grip on his own gun that had been shaking in his hand inside his pocket. He exhaled the breath he'd been holding.

Milo hit the street and put the Mercedes in drive then waited as the suited man pocketed his gun and slid behind the wheel of the two-door. As soon as the engine turned over Milo gassed Hugh's car away on a pre-designated route. He had begun his final exam in the college of McGraw.

By the time the suited man had reversed down the drive and started to chase, Tucker and Calvin were already on their way back to the truck. When they arrived back at the front door each carrying a box of cash Hugh Stanley himself had made it halfway down the stairs, pulling on a robe.

"Oh, good. You're up," Calvin said.

"What the fuck is this?" Hugh demanded.

Tucker dropped his box and raised the gun. "Shut up and sit down."

Hugh lifted his hands and glanced around, wondering if he should sit there on the bottom step.

"In here," Calvin said, and led them all in to the family room. The large room fit two couches comfortably around a large fireplace. Tucker switched on an overhead light fixture as they stepped in and Calvin placed the box of money he carried on an antique coffee table with dovetailing.

"You two wait here and chat while I get the rest, huh?" Calvin seemed to be enjoying his part in all this. He certainly was better than Tucker at speaking up. Tucker didn't know what to say and any thoughts he had were crowded out by the details of the plan cycling through his head over and over like a washer on spin cycle. Frankly, he hadn't expected to make it this far.

He didn't say a word to Hugh in the time it took Calvin to stack all eleven banker's boxes in the living room before the burgundy velvet couch Hugh sat in, his robe cinched tight and his feet stuffed into lambswool slippers.

Earlier, as they were detailing the plan, Calvin had explained to Tucker and Milo about Hugh Stanley's ex-wife. About ten years before she had finally gotten sick of his sleeping around with younger women. Her wrath came to a head after Hugh contracted genital warts and gave them to her. She tried to use that as grounds for divorce and even went as far as to hire a lawyer. Three weeks later she went missing and her body was never found, headless or otherwise.

Hugh lived alone in the house ever since, a chef in the mornings and a single bodyguard his only companions.

"So you know what this is, right?" Calvin said as he tapped

a finger on a three-box stack.

"You brought me my money back. About time." Hugh eyeballed the stacks. "Seem to be one short."

"Had to, uh, pay off a certain someone. Couldn't be avoided."

"I see."

Tucker kept the revolver at hip level, aiming at the seated man. "We went to see Kirby, you know."

"Did you now?"

"Yes, we did." Tucker grew bolder as Hugh grew more arrogant. "Your theory that he was the one who killed my dad, that's kind of out the window, huh?"

"I guess so."

"So it was you."

Hugh crossed his legs like he was waiting to be served tea. "I haven't killed anyone in thirty years."

Calvin lifted the lid on the box nearest him. "Oh, we met the man who pulled the trigger. He done blowed up though." Calvin grinned as he lifted two stacks on bills out of the box. He walked over to the fireplace and with his foot, turned a key that started a slow hiss of gas. "You got any matches around here?"

Hugh swallowed. Calvin did a quick scan of the mantle area and found a fancy wooden box in Chinese lacquer. He opened the box and inside were stacks of long matches like chopsticks with tiny blue tips. He lifted one out and struck it against the stone mantle. A flame sparked to life.

Calvin turned to Hugh as he tossed the lit match behind the fireplace screen. The built-up gas ignited with a whoomp and the blast of heat moved through the room like the ghost of fires past. A pile of fake logs glowed orange.

"So we're guessing you need this money pretty bad. Good plan, by the way, laundering through Canada."

"It's not laundered. It's a loan. It's not even my money. You do anything foolish and you'll be pissing off a hell of a lot more people than just me and mine."

Calvin raised his money-filled hands to his face and made a faux scared face. "Ohhh, Canadians. Look out. I'm so terrified, eh?" He finished his performance with a laugh.

Hugh clenched his jaw. Calvin tossed the two stacks of cash into the fire then opened his empty hands as if the money had vanished and he had no idea how.

Tucker tipped over a box and dozens of tightly wrapped bundles of money spilled onto the Oriental rug. "You see, we're not going to kill you."

"Unless you make us," Calvin clarified.

"We're not that kind of guys. You thought we'd kill that guy you sent into the woods, but we didn't. You did, but that wasn't our fault. That's not to say we don't want you to suffer."

Tucker bent down and scooped up eight stacks of money and dumped them into the fire like coal into a train engine. The bundles caught quickly and burned bright.

"You see," Calvin said as he picked up three bundles in each hand. "You can shit on us McGraws for a good many years, as you have done. You can pay us less than we're worth. You can put us in harms way. Truth of it is, we'd do the work for free, it's so damn fun. But you had to go and kill one of us." He tossed his load into the fire. "Your biggest mistake though, Hugh. You didn't kill all of us."

Calvin kicked out and toppled the stack of three boxes. Tucker overturned two more. The floor became piled with green bricks of hundred dollar bills. In the flush times the pile would have been to fuck three or four underage girls on top of. Right then, it looked like piles of thick green vomit all over his $20,000 rug.

It became a game, a little competition between Tucker and Calvin to see who could scoop the money into the fire faster. The men smiled and Tucker had a fleeting memory of a snowball fight when he was seven years old.

The men were so focused on the burning of the money that Hugh saw an opening and lunged forward from the couch to make a grab at Tucker.

The gun still in his hand, Tucker turned and shot, catching Hugh in the foot and dropping him immediately face-down onto a pile of money.

Calvin and Tucker both helped him back onto the couch then went back to their task, ignoring his moaning and the clenching of his foot. Those lambswool slippers were ruined.

Calvin held the last stack of hundreds. He looked at the bulging fire, the flames threatening to overrun the fire screen. He reached out the stack and offered it to Tucker, giving him the honors. Tucker stepped up and threw the last of Hugh Stanley's millions onto the pile to burn.

Grandson and Grandfather exchanged a look of pride in accomplishment and Tucker began thinking about phase two of the plan: get the fuck out of Iowa.

At any other time in his life Calvin relished the sound of tires squealing. Right then, it meant trouble.

31

Tucker's mind had been sufficiently preoccupied that he hadn't allowed himself to think about his son out driving around being chased by a gun-wielding thug. The scream of rubber on the driveway brought Milo back to the forefront of his thoughts.

If the commotion was his son returning to drive them all away then the plan had worked, if not then it could mean something awful. He didn't have time to dwell on possibilities before more pressing issues once again spun his mind to focus on only what was right in front of him.

Heavy footfalls sounded in the hallway after the front door came crashing in. Tucker tightened his grip on the .38 in his fist, but it felt quite small and he wouldn't have been surprised at all if he pulled the trigger and a flag with the word BANG! came flopping out.

Four of Stanley's suited men came thundering into the room. Each held a gun in their hand.

As if he only had one chance left to do it, Calvin reached down and punched Hugh across the jaw. The snapping bone sound reached Tucker's ears a second before the first gunshot.

Lost in the sudden explosion of gunfire was Calvin saying, "That felt good."

Calvin fell to a knee and slipped around the side of the couch as two bullets joined the party with Hugh's foot injury. The new shots were to his chest and from a much larger gun. Hugh slumped flat on the couch, running out of places on his body to clutch in pain.

Tucker ran for the second couch, but had to come forward to make it around the high arm and nearly ran into one of the gunmen charging forward. Whatever they had been told to get them to come out to Hugh's place they were prepared for much more of an army than an octogenarian and his insurance salesman grandson.

In a very short time they had fired enough bullets to drop a SWAT team, but Calvin and Tucker made such small targets they had gotten away unharmed.

Tucker found himself bumping into a young man with a shaved head and a tattoo on his neck of some gothic symbol Tucker didn't know the meaning of. Tucker clamped his arm down over the young man's gun hand, pinning it between Tucker's chest and arm. He spun and the man had no choice but to spin with him. Tucker lifted his arm at the apex of the turn and like a ballet dancer the young man spun off and did a full rotation before crashing through the fire screen.

A bullet came past Tucker close enough that he felt the wind move on his cheek. He ducked and fired the .38 blindly. His tiny bullet caught the kneecap of the suited man shooting at him and the man cried out.

From out of the fire the shaved headed man stood, his jacket burning. He slapped at his head and his ears as he tried to get his arms out of the flaming suit coat. He ran forward, dropping the jacket on the oriental rug as he aimed himself like a torpedo out of the room. He blasted into the chest of one of the two remaining standing men, who both watched the human torch with slack jaws.

The not-on-fire man whuffed out all the air from his lungs as the shaved head of the first man punched into his stomach. The 9mm he carried bounced quietly on the rug and he went down with it.

The shaved-headed man stumbled out of the room still slapping at any exposed skin on his body putting out sparks and embers that clung to his flesh. As they burned, the deeper they scorched him, the more stubborn they were to remove.

Calvin reached for the dropped 9mm and fired two shots into the ceiling over the lone standing gunman. He threw his hands up over his head as if the plaster dust was the most dangerous thing in the room, never mind the loaded weapons and open flames, before he turned and ran back out.

Tucker stepped to the couch and peered over Hugh Stanley's writhing body to Calvin on the floor behind the sofa.

"You okay?"

"Yeah, you?"

"For now."

Tucker looked down to see the flaming jacket becoming a fire you'd want to roast marshmallows over.

Outside a car horn sounded. Three times in rapid succession. Milo's signal.

Tucker looked from the fire spreading around the room to Stanley on the couch. "Guess we're even now."

Hugh Stanley could say nothing. His lungs struggled to find breath, his jaw hung loose.

Tucker held out a hand and Calvin took it. The two men

227

rushed out of the room.

Back in the hall, Tucker was struck by how much cooler it was. The heat from the fire had been building slowly as they added stack after stack of money and he hadn't noticed how hot the room had become. Now as they ran toward the open front door he felt the six A.M. cool from outside.

Whether the men on Hugh's rescue team thought they were outnumbered or simply hadn't fully woken up yet after whatever 5 A.M. emergency call they'd gotten, Tucker was grateful they'd turned out to be such idiots. He understood a little of why the McGraw men had been such a valuable commodity over the years. Reliable, good at their job and took pride in the work. A rare combination these days, especially in the crime world.

The Mercedes was a welcome sight. Angled across the lawn with two thick black gashes carved out of the grass behind it. Calvin had never been more happy to get into a German car.

The passenger door already stood open and Milo beckoned them from inside. Calvin slid in and Tucker opened the door to the back seat. Before his door was shut Milo had the tires spinning on the dew-covered lawn.

"Everyone okay?" he asked.

"Everyone that matters," Calvin said.

Milo controlled the wild fishtail of the Mercedes' back end as the tires gained grip on the wet grass. Two new cars were parked in the driveway, Hugh's rescue squad. Calvin did hope they got him out of the burning house. At least so he could suffer through the healing of his broken jaw. He smiled to himself as he rubbed the knuckles of his right hand.

Milo bumped the Mercedes onto the street and they were

met by the shrill whine of sirens and the red and blue flashes of police cruisers in the pre-sunrise gray.

"Shit." Milo spun the car and the tires chirped along the pavement as he gunned the engine in the opposite direction. Calvin almost blurted out driving advice, but he didn't see anything he would change about how the boy was doing.

"How you feeling there, boy?"

"It's better than pussy." A wide grin joined the intense look on concentration on Milo's face.

"Let's not get carried away now."

Tucker slid from one side of the back seat across to the other as he struggled to get a grip on a belt that would fix him to the seat.

One police cruiser angled into Stanley's driveway while the other continued on after the Mercedes.

Calvin secured his own belt. "Well, Milo. You're really going from zero to McGraw in one shot tonight. Tell you what, cops and our family are like magnets and wood—they don't stick. Lose this son of a bitch and we'll add your name to the wall of honor."

Milo blasted through a stop sign in the quiet suburban neighborhood. A sprinkler cut on in a yard as they barreled past.

The persistent siren clung to them like body odor. Milo took a sharp right turn, the back end swinging out and squealing tires. The cop car followed. Ahead, a station wagon with fake wood panels cruised slowly down the middle of the street straddling the hashed yellow lines. Every other house a newspaper would sail out the open windows from one side or the other to slap like a dead fish on the lawn of a subscription holder.

Milo hugged the right curb, recalculated the space he had then swung over to the left curb. Neither would be enough. The wagon drooled along no faster than a bike, how the job used to be done, and Milo had to brake hard to avoid driving up his tailpipe.

"To the right. Fewer trees," Calvin said.

Milo cut the wheel and aimed the Mercedes into a driveway then veered off across the front lawn, crushing a newspaper under a tire as he went. The police car paused behind the wagon and waited for it to pull to the side like an obedient taxpayer.

Milo crossed flower beds and one weedy overgrown lawn before he turned a sharp left and leapt the curb back into the street, clipping a mailbox as he went.

"Good job, boy. Every teenage boy needs to take out a mailbox at some point."

They'd managed to put an extra block between them and the police car, but the siren still stuck solid to their bumper.

"What do I do?"

"We wait for an opportunity to present itself," Calvin said.

"Parking lot!" Tucker said. "Over there."

The residential street ran out at the end of the block and a supermarket stood at the corner framed by a liquor store and a dry cleaners and fronted with a sprawling parking lot. Milo aimed the Mercedes toward it.

"Parking lots I can do."

Through another stop sign he drove across four lanes of a crosstown street and scraped the front end on the incline as they entered the nearly empty lot. The supermarket was 24 hours so a small cluster of cars grouped near the entrance, but otherwise the area was a wide open expanse of empty spots divided by medians, light poles, shopping cart corrals and the occasional stray cart that had wandered away from the corral.

"I'm not sure this is a good idea," Calvin said.

"I'm open to better ones," Milo said as he wove the Mercedes in and out of the aisles.

The police car followed and chased Milo down as he carved out a maze through the white lines, around the medians, looped around forty-foot light poles before starting all over again at the other end of the lot.

The cop car was so close now Calvin could see the angry faces of the two officers inside. He thanked God for small towns with little or no backup, especially at six A.M. when the budgets had wreaked havoc on overtime and night pay.

Milo maintained meticulous control befitting the German automobile as he snaked through the maze again, creating his own pattern of hairpins turns and cutbacks.

Tucker began to feel queasy.

The police car came tantalizingly close and the smell of blood in the water made him try for several moves out of the cop manual. He tried to get a bumper on the rear panel of the Mercedes and force him into a spin, but Calvin saw the attempt coming and warned Milo to swerve.

He tried to anticipate a turn and aimed to be there when Milo made his move, but again Calvin noticed the change in follow patterns and warned his great-grandson.

"Okay, I'm about done with this shit," Calvin said. "Milo, when you get to the end of this row cut over two and when I say the word you turn as hard a right turn as you can in this Nazi can of bolts."

"Okay."

"Here you go now. Listen to me and do what I say."

Tucker grabbed hold of the strap above the door. Something in him felt it would be a good idea.

Behind them, the cop car made the screeching turn and followed down the row of empty spaces.

"Good. Now three... two... one... turn."

Milo cut the wheel all the way right as Calvin pulled up hard on the handbrake. The Mercedes spun in a tight circle Calvin was grudgingly impressed with and wound up facing back toward the police cruiser.

Calvin dropped the hand brake back down. "Gun it."

Milo did. The Mercedes accelerated toward the cop car which squealed its tires as the anti-lock brakes struggled to hold.

"Now ease off."

Milo did. The Mercedes bumped noses with the cop car and the jolt sent all three men tightening against their seat belts.

"Now, full throttle. Push him into that light post."

The eight-cylinder engine growled as it pushed the police car backwards, the two men inside disoriented and struggling to turn and see where they were being forced to go. After the long chase the brakes on the cop car were spent and did little to stop them from being pushed.

"Don't let up yet."

Milo closed one eye as the impact approached.

"Now, brake!" Again Calvin pulled up on the handbrake as Milo stomped on the pedal. The Mercedes still crashed into the front end of the cop car as it backed into the pole, but the damage was minimal.

Calvin swung open his door and fired two shots at the left front tire only a few feet away from him. The cops inside ducked. The tire popped and hissed.

"Now get us out of here," he said as he slammed the door.

Milo reversed, spun the wheel and moved into drive as he raced away from the supermarket towards home.

A mile away, Calvin spotted another car parked along the curb on a slow residential street. They parked the Mercedes, got out and Tucker bent over a bush in the front yard and threw up.

While Tucker puked, Calvin broke into the Buick. Not his first choice but at least it was American.

32

Three generations of McGraws entered the house of the fourth, missing, generation. They stumbled inside a little like soldiers returning from the front line and a little like frat boys after an all-nighter.

"How long do you think we have?" Tucker asked.

Calvin sucked in a deep breath, thinking it over. "I think we're okay on time. They don't seem to have guessed we're staying here. Your house is already burned down. Plus, I think we left a hell of a mess to clean up back there. I think Hugh isn't going to be making any decisions anytime soon. If he even makes it, that is."

Tucker eyed the couch, but wouldn't let himself sit. Too much to do.

"Who wants some breakfast?"

"Me," Milo said. He helped his dad make scrambled eggs and bacon. The men ate in near silence, each one planning their next move. Picking up and leaving town forever wasn't as simple as Tucker had thought it would be.

He made some phone calls to Annabelle and broke the news that he would be shutting down the office. He asked her to box up his documents and he would send for them at a later date. She sounded highly suspicious of everything he said, but she let him go without any questions. Also without a formal goodbye since she thought there was no way he could actually be leaving for good.

Calvin placed a single suitcase by the door. He took the keys to the Bandit down from the hook.

"It'll be good to feel the old girl grab my ass cheeks again."

Tucker smiled. The list of unfinished business grew every time he thought about it. He stopped himself before he spiraled into doubt. He thought very hard and nearly everything fell away from the list.

Business? Check. House? Not a problem. He'd have a new address to send the insurance check soon. Car? He'd just inherited Webb's.

His son was with him. His dad's killer had been found, and dealt with.

One nagging thing stuck with him. He found Milo in the kitchen making peanut butter sandwiches for the road. He spoke to him quietly, so Calvin wouldn't hear.

"Did your mom leave you a phone number?"

"A cell phone, Dad. She asked me not to even tell you about it."

Tucker nodded. "But, she said she'd be in touch?"

"Yeah."

"That's good. You shouldn't lose her forever. And, Milo, don't blame her. She did what she thought was right."

"Yeah, I guess."

"Trust me. I can speak from experience. Now, anyway."

They all met at the front door.

"So we're taking three cars?" Milo asked.

"I'm in the Bandit," Calvin said. "Tuck, what are you driving?"

"I guess I'll take the Barracuda and Milo can take the GSX."

"Sweet."

"And you better appreciate it, boy. I don't want you fantasizing about a damn European car or something."

Tucker turned and took in the living room of his childhood home for the last time.

"You know, I have to say, and please don't give me any crap for this" Tucker turned back to Calvin and Milo. "I'm feeling like burning all that money wasn't the smartest move. I'll get a decent settlement from the house, but it sure would be nice to have the cash right about now when everything is so uncertain."

Calvin and Milo exchanged a look. They both tried to hide slight smiles. Tucker caught their conspiracy. "What?"

"Well, Tuck, we didn't exactly burn all the money."

Tucker stared them down like a scolding parent.

"We kinda kept some of it."

"How much?" Tucker directed the question at Milo, knowing he would be more likely to get a straight answer.

Calvin bent down and thumbed open the latch on his suitcase. "Two million," he said and let the case drop open exposing one half packed with socks and boxer shorts and the other half filled with tidy rows of cash.

"How did you...?"

"We took a few stacks out of each box. That way there were still eleven boxes left and Hugh, and you, wouldn't know there was any missing."

Tucker looked at Milo, accusing. "And you knew about this?"

"Kinda."

Tucker shook his head, a smile growing on his face. "Jesus Christ. Granddad, how many times in all this did you save me from myself?"

"Hey now, you saved my ass plenty. You really proved you were a McGraw after all." Calvin put a hand on Milo's shoulder. "And this one saved all our asses. The boy's got a gift. We need to nurture it."

"Nurture it right into college you mean. You can consider a big chunk of that money already spent."

"You're gonna let all that natural talent go to waste?"

"He can drive you to the store for beer."

"Then it's not a complete waste."

The men shared a laugh. Tucker lifted the handle on his suitcase first. Calvin shut his and hefted the heavy case. Milo held his modest bag.

"To Omaha?" Tucker asked.

"For now," Calvin answered.

Tucker pulled on the door and opened it to find a figure on the stoop. He jumped a little at the man standing before him.

Ambrose.

Six feet behind him on the lawn were two of his cousins, one with a hand wrapped in thick bandages. They took a slight step back when the door opened.

"You. What the hell do you want?"

Calvin dropped his suitcase and filled the doorframe next to Tucker. "We don't have your car anymore, man. You need to get the fuck out of here."

Ambrose held up his open palms in surrender. "I'm not here about the car. I don't want any trouble."

"Then what the fuck are you here for?"

Tucker braced for a gunshot or the click of a switchblade being pulled.

"I want to hire you."

Tucker and Calvin blinked. "What?"

"I have some people who owe me money. When you came to collect from me I tried to collect from them, but they wouldn't give me what they owed me. I thought, perhaps, you could get it for me."

Tucker looked over Ambrose's shoulder to the two figures on the lawn. "What about your cousins there?"

"I've come to the opinion that you are more... persuasive than they are."

Tucker turned to Calvin. They thought for a moment. Calvin turned back to Ambrose. "Hang on a minute."

He closed the door. The two men stood in the entryway with Milo looking on, again in the role of wondering what was going to happen.

"What do you say?" Calvin asked. "One more job?"

"But, we're not collectors or whatever. I told you before, I'm not a criminal."

Calvin placed his hand on Tucker's shoulder, dropped his eyes and spoke to him slow and low. "Tuck, you got to can it with that shit. You are what you are and what you are is a McGraw. No, we ain't criminals." He paused, waiting for Tucker to fill the gap.

"We're outlaws." Tucker turned to Milo. "Unpack. We're staying a while longer."

Calvin smiled, feeling younger than he had in decades.

About the Author

Eric Beetner is the author of The Devil Doesn't Want Me, Dig Two Graves, The Year I Died Seven Times, White Hot Pistol, Stripper Pole At the End Of The World, the story collection A Bouquet Of Bullets, co-author (with JB Kohl) of the novels One Too Many Blows To The Head and Borrowed Trouble, and he has written the novellas FIGHTCARD: Split Decision and FIGHTCARD: A Mouth Full Of Blood under the name Jack Tunney.

He lives in Los Angeles where he co-hosts the Noir At The Bar reading series.

CPSIA information can be obtained
at www.ICGtesting.com
Printed in the USA
FSOW01n0956210515
7329FS